THE UNSEEN WORLD OF
Poppy Malone
A Mischief of Mermaids

The Unseen World of
Poppy Malone
A Mischief of Mermaids

Suzanne Harper

Greenwillow Books
An Imprint of HarperCollins*Publishers*

The Unseen World of Poppy Malone: A Mischief of Mermaids
Copyright © 2013 by Suzanne Harper

All rights reserved. No part of this book may be used or reproduced in any manner whatsoever without written permission except in the case of brief quotations embodied in critical articles and reviews. Printed in the United States of America. For information address HarperCollins Children's Books, a division of HarperCollins Publishers, 10 East 53rd Street, New York, NY 10022.
www.harpercollinschildrens.com

The text of this book is set in 12-point ITC Esprit.
Book design by Paul Zakris

Library of Congress Cataloging-in-Publication Data

Harper, Suzanne.
A mischief of mermaids / by Suzanne Harper.
pages cm.—(The unseen world of Poppy Malone)
Summary: Nearly-ten-year-old Poppy Malone finds her skepticism challenged again when she must deal with troublemakers at Lake Travis who look and act suspiciously like mermaids, which she knows do not exist.
ISBN 978-0-06-199613-9 (hardback)
[1. Mermaids—Fiction. 2. Family life—Texas—Fiction. 3. Brothers and sisters—Fiction. 4. Twins—Fiction. 5. Houseboats—Fiction. 6. Travis, Lake (Tex.)—Fiction.] I. Title.
PZ7.H23197Mis 2013 [Fic]—dc23 2012046725

13 14 15 16 17 LP/RRDH 10 9 8 7 6 5 4 3 2 1
First Edition

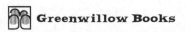 **Greenwillow Books**

For all the mischief makers

THE UNSEEN WORLD OF
Poppy Malone
A Mischief of Mermaids

Chapter ONE

"**I** have one very important question to ask you." Professor Oliver Asquith's searching gaze swept over the Malone family. He lowered his voice. *"Are you afraid?"*

Poppy sighed. Her eyes slid sideways to meet Will's. She raised one eyebrow. He wrinkled his nose.

Maybe it was because they were twins (both counting down the days until their tenth birthday), but they each knew exactly what the other was thinking:

It was too good to last.

It had been nice of Oliver Asquith to invite them to spend the day on the houseboat that a television network had rented for him. They had had fun swimming in the lake, sunning themselves on the deck, and eating the delicious food served by the private catering staff that came with the boat. But the best part, Poppy thought, was that no one had talked about anything weird or spooky all day.

This was highly unusual, because Oliver Asquith, like her parents, was a paranormal investigator. When they got together, all they could talk about was vampires, werewolves, fairies, and dozens of other creatures that most sensible people didn't believe in.

But today, for a few brief, blessed hours, the conversation had actually been normal, thanks to Mrs. Malone.

As they were getting ready to go on board earlier that day, she had said to Mr. Malone, "Now, let's not spoil what could be a lovely day by arguing."

"I don't know what you're talking about," he had said. "Oliver and I never argue. You can't call an honest, open exchange of ideas an argument. And we have always followed the rules of civil debate. Always."

Poppy and Will had rolled their eyes at each other. Over the years, they had heard quite a few of those "honest, open exchanges of ideas." They usually ended with raised voices, slammed doors, and fists thumping on tables, which was sometimes interesting and always entertaining, but hardly civil.

The problem was that Oliver Asquith made a much better living than their parents and was much, much more famous.

Mr. and Mrs. Malone had spent years scraping by with grants and short-term teaching jobs. When the grants ended and the teaching contracts were over, they would often have to move across the country in search of more money. Oliver Asquith, on the other hand, had managed to turn his search for vampires, zombies, and werewolves into both fortune and fame. He wrote best-selling books, starred in TV specials, and had even created a paranormal kit with his picture on it that was sold in drugstores nationwide.

Mr. Malone tried to take all this in stride, but it was a struggle.

Now he said with some heat, "The only time I argue with Oliver Asquith is when he's wrong. I'll admit that's most of the time—"

"This is exactly what I'm talking about," said Mrs. Malone severely. "He is our host, Emerson. We must all try to be polite."

"Well, I can't help it if he insists on saying ridiculous things," said Mr. Malone. "Did you hear him last night? Claiming that he saw water nymphs frolicking in a spring on his last visit to Greece? He either had a bad case of sunstroke or he's started hallucinating again—"

Mrs. Malone sighed. "Just change the subject, dear, to something you can agree on. That's all I ask."

Mr. Malone had grumpily agreed. He had been sorely tested when they arrived at the boat, however.

"Welcome to the *Siren de Mer*!" Oliver Asquith had said. "Come, let me give you a tour."

The Malones had dutifully followed him. Oliver Asquith had told them about the houseboat when he invited them, of course, so they were ready to be impressed. But even so, their eyes were wide by the time they were walking around the deck to admire the barbecue grill and hot tub. When Oliver pointed out the waterslide that stretched from the crow's nest to the water—or the kayaks and Jet Skis nestled in cradles on deck—Poppy thought she could hear Mr. Malone's teeth grinding.

They trailed after him as he led them below deck. "Four bedrooms, a gourmet kitchen, and a fifty-inch flat-screen TV! With surround sound, of course—" Oliver Asquith stopped walking and turned to face them, his eyes bright. "Oh, and did I mention the satellite cable?"

"I think it's come up once or twice," muttered Mr. Malone. "If memory serves."

"And of course there's the Jacuzzi," Oliver added.

"But no bathtub," said Poppy's older sister, Franny. "You'd think a boat this big would have at least one bathtub."

"Who cares?" said Will. "There's a *waterslide*!"

"It's true, there's no bathtub," admitted Oliver,

with a smile that managed to seem weary but brave. "Traveling around the world to host top-rated TV specials is a grueling life. One must be willing to rough it a bit."

Mr. Malone made a small sound in the back of his throat. From where Poppy stood, it sounded like a stifled groan.

Still, Mr. Malone recovered enough to follow Mrs. Malone's directive. After the tour, Poppy and Will swam in the lake and Franny sunned herself on the deck and their younger brother, Rolly, stood moodily in the bow, dropping pieces of gravel he had been collecting from neighbors' driveways into the water. For several hours, they all enjoyed themselves while Mr. and Mrs. Malone and Oliver Asquith talked in a most civil fashion.

They had discussed the best sunblock to use while traveling in the Amazon rain forest in search of Mapinguari. They had debated whether it was better to take cheese sandwiches or corned beef on a Sasquatch stakeout. They had traded tips on the best insect repellent to use in the South China Sea.

It had all been remarkably boring, and Poppy couldn't have been happier. Boredom, she thought, was highly underrated. Boredom gave you lots of time to think and wonder and dream up inventions. And boredom was relaxing.

Then Oliver Asquith had ruined it all by deciding to show off.

"I must practice the opening for my new TV special," he said. "Would you mind . . . would it be too much trouble . . . could I ask an enormous favor—?"

"Say no more," said Mrs. Malone brightly. "We'd love to be your audience!"

"Thank you, that's most generous of you. And of course I'd like to hear any feedback about how I can spruce things up a bit," said Oliver Asquith, smiling modestly. "That's the downside of having filmed more than a dozen immensely popular shows, I'm afraid. There are millions of people around the world who are expecting me to top myself."

"Count me as one of the ones who wants to see that," muttered Mr. Malone. *"Ow."*

Mrs. Malone whipped off her sunglasses, the better to glare at him. "We are all most interested in hearing you, Oliver," she said. "Aren't we, Emerson?"

"Of course," he said, rubbing his ankle where she had kicked him. "In fact, we're on the edge of our seats."

Poppy could tell Mr. Malone was being sarcastic. If Oliver Asquith noticed Mr. Malone's tone, however, he ignored it.

Instead, he leaned casually against the railing. A breeze ruffled his wavy hair and his blue eyes sparkled as he addressed an unseen camera.

He cleared his throat and said again, "I have a very important question to ask you. Are you afraid? Because if you aren't afraid"—he paused dramatically as Mr. Malone rolled his eyes—"you should be."

Oliver Asquith knew how to read an audience's reactions. In this case, it ranged from unimpressed (Poppy) to amused (Will) to adoring (thirteen-year-old Franny) to disgruntled (Mr. Malone) to encouraging (Mrs. Malone) to baleful (five-year-old Rolly).

Oliver Asquith rightly decided to focus on Franny and Mrs. Malone.

"You should be *very* afraid. Because"—he lowered his voice ominously—"Here There Be Monsters!"

There was a short pause. In the silence, Poppy could hear the distant roar of a Jet Ski. When that faded away, the only sound left was water lapping against the side of the boat.

Then Mr. Malone could no longer restrain himself. "Lake monsters?" he said. "Really, Oliver? That's what you've sold to a national TV network? No one cares about lake monsters these days—*oof!*"

Mr. Malone was interrupted—knocked out of his deck chair, as a matter of fact—by his younger son, Rolly, who had run over to the railing and leaned perilously over the side.

"Where are they?" he demanded, his beady black eyes scanning the lake. "Where are the monsters?"

"Well," said Oliver Asquith in a gloating voice, "it looks as if at least one potential viewer is still enthralled by the subject."

Mr. Malone gingerly got to his feet and righted his deck chair. "Yes," he said through gritted teeth. "And if you're hoping for an audience of five-year-olds, I'll admit you've got a chance. But otherwise—"

"Rolly, dear, be careful!" said Mrs. Malone, grabbing him by the back of his shirt and pulling him away from the railing. "You might fall in the water."

Rolly wrested himself out of her grasp. "I don't care! I want to see the monster!"

"Yes, and so will everyone else who tunes in," said Mr. Malone. "How about it, Oliver? Have you managed to shoot any footage of this lake monster yet? Any *usable* footage, I should say?"

Oliver Asquith smiled blandly. "My investigation is still in its infancy, but the early signs are quite promising," he said. "And, of course, there is still so much to discover—"

"No, in other words." Mr. Malone sat down again, smiling with satisfaction.

"I would not say 'no,'" Oliver Asquith said. "I would say 'not yet.'"

Rolly turned around and fixed his eyes accusingly on Oliver Asquith. "You *said* there was a monster," said Rolly. His lower lip began to stick out in a dangerous way that everyone in his family was familiar with. "You *said* there was one in this lake—"

"There's no such thing as lake monsters, Rolly," Poppy said. "Professor Asquith was just having a little fun."

"I wouldn't dismiss the idea too quickly, dear," warned Mrs. Malone, even as she tightened her grip on Rolly's arm. "After all, there have been documented sightings of lake monsters all around the world, going back for centuries! There's Memprhe in Canada—"

"Brosnie in Russia," added Oliver Asquith.

"The Hucho taimen in China," continued Mrs. Malone. "Over the centuries, people have reported seeing all kinds of strange beasts in lakes and ponds and oceans. They've seen creatures that looked like dinosaurs or giant snakes or even horses!"

"They were probably just giant catfish," said Poppy. "Or submerged logs. Or unusual wave patterns."

"Still the skeptic, I see, Poppy," said Oliver Asquith in an amused voice that made Poppy want to push him over the railing.

"Still the scientist," she corrected him.

He smiled a flashing smile at her, completely unruffled. "Fortunately," he said in a voice as rich as cream, "others are not as rational as you. That's why I was able to sign a very lucrative contract for my new TV special. That's why the network was willing to rent a houseboat that offers every comfort so that I could really concentrate on my work. That's why I have not one, not two, but three assistants at my beck and call."

By this time, Mr. Malone was pale with envy, but he mustered enough spirit to say, "By the way, where are your assistants, Oliver? When I didn't see any young graduate students hanging about, I assumed that you had suffered another one of those sad accidents that seem to happen to you so often."

"What do you mean by that?" For the first time, Oliver sounded testy.

"Well, you don't have much luck with your assistants, do you?" said Mr. Malone, his eyes gleaming with triumph. "I mean, there was the young man who was decapitated by a vampire in Moldavia, and then the girl with the orange-and-purple hair, what was her name—"

"Naomi," supplied Mrs. Malone. "Such a dear little thing."

"Mm, yes," said Mr. Malone. "A dear little thing who ended up in the hospital after being bitten by an enormous dog—"

"Werewolf," Oliver said automatically. "And she's actually quite proud of that scar."

"And then there was that boy who hunted ghosts for you—"

"Sam," Will said. "I liked him. He told really cool stories. Like that one about the guy that had his head cut off in some old castle and kept haunting it and throwing his head down the halls like a bowling ball—"

"Yes, he was quite enthusiastic. I remember how excited he was about spending the night in that former insane asylum with his infrared camera." Mr. Malone shook his head sadly. "Has anyone ever found any trace of him? Or of his infrared camera?"

"Not yet," Oliver said with a tight smile. "The network set up a scholarship in his name, of course. And since no body was ever found, I still hold out hope. . . ."

Poppy chose this moment to stand up and wander away.

She flopped on her stomach near the edge of the deck and closed her eyes, enjoying the feel of sun on her back. The sound of Oliver Asquith's voice, as well as that of Mr. and Mrs. Malones', became a distant murmur. As long as she didn't have to listen to his nonsense, she was able to relax and think her own, far more interesting thoughts.

Every once in a while, though, a word or

phrase would seem to get caught by the breeze and float over to her—she distinctly heard "prehistoric creature," "thirty feet long," and "unexplained disappearance"—and she would feel herself getting annoyed again.

It was ridiculous to think that monsters could live in a lake like this without being discovered. Maybe a hundred years ago, but not now, not in the twenty-first century.

If any of the sightings were real, surely a marine biologist would have done a search by now, using sonar or something. And if scientists weren't interested in tracking down a monster, a TV reporter would be. There was just no way that a mysterious creature could remain a mystery for very long in this day and age. . . .

These thoughts were so pleasant, and the sound of the waves splashing gently against the hull was so soothing, and the sun was so warm, that Poppy felt herself drifting off to sleep.

Lake monsters, she thought drowsily. What a silly idea . . .

And then, just as she was about to fall asleep, she heard a giggle.

Poppy sighed. Franny had recently developed an annoying habit of giggling when she was around a boy she liked. The most recent incident, which had been very embarrassing, had occurred at an ice-cream shop downtown where a teen boy was making sundaes by dramatically flipping scoops of ice cream in the air and then catching them in a dish held behind his back. Franny had been so taken with this performance that Will had finally poured a cup of ice water down the back of her shirt to stop her from going into full-fledged hysterics.

Poppy opened one eye a tiny slit and turned her head toward the other side of the houseboat, where Oliver Asquith was holding court. If Franny had started giggling at Oliver Asquith, Poppy thought, she might have to push her overboard.

But Franny was sitting in a deck chair near the bow, lost in contemplation of her newly painted toenails (bright pink on the toes of her left foot and bright green on the right).

Poppy shrugged and closed her eyes.

Then she heard the giggle again, followed by the sound of a splash.

She didn't open her eyes, but a small frown appeared on her forehead.

Then drops of water landed on her face.

Poppy sat up, glaring around the deck. If Will thought it was funny to wake her up by throwing water on her—

But Will was leaning against the railing on the other side of the houseboat, drinking a soda.

That's when Poppy realized what had bothered her about that giggle.

It sounded like it came from under the boat. It sounded, in fact, like it came from the bottom of the lake.

Chapter
TWO

Poppy leaned over the side of the boat and stared into the water. All she saw were some bits of lake weed waving to and fro, a fish flashing by, and an empty soda can bobbing on the surface.

She wrinkled her nose.

Well, sounds travel in strange ways over water, she thought. Everyone knew that. She had probably heard someone laughing on a nearby boat.

And yet . . .

Poppy frowned. There had been something odd about that giggle. It wasn't the giggle of someone who was laughing at a joke. It had sounded almost . . . musical, like chimes ringing underwater—

At that moment, Oliver Asquith's cell phone

rang, interrupting her thoughts. Poppy knew it was his because the ring tone was the theme song from *The X-Files* and because it had been ringing constantly ever since they had come on board.

Every time the phone rang, he would make an apologetic face at the Malones and say, "I'm sorry, but I really have to take this. I'll just be a moment." Then he would sit in a deck chair positioned so that he could watch Mr. Malone's face as he loudly talked to film and TV producers, book publishers, and even celebrities (a very famous movie star was interested in playing Oliver in a movie about his paranormal adventures).

Poppy squeezed her eyes shut so she couldn't see Oliver Asquith's smug face. She wished she could put her fingers in her ears so she didn't have to listen to him, either, but she knew that would be rude.

"What?" she heard Oliver say. "But that's incredible! It's been years since the last eyewitness sighting of the Loch Ness Monster!"

She turned her head in order to see him.

Professor Asquith was pacing back and forth on the deck. One hand held his cell phone to his ear, while the other ran through his thick, TV-ready hair.

As he listened, he glanced at Mr. and Mrs. Malone, his face alive with excitement. "It's my assistant, the graduate student I sent to Scotland," he whispered, pointing to the phone. "She's spotted Nessie!"

"Oh, how wonderful for you!" Mrs. Malone seemed genuinely pleased about Oliver's good fortune. "It's such a thrilling moment when one finally sees a creature one has been hunting for so long, isn't it, Emerson!"

"Oliver hasn't seen it," said Mr. Malone. "His assistant has."

"Yes, and she's taken a photo, too!" Oliver Asquith turned his phone around so that they could see its screen. Franny and Will crowded next to Oliver to peer at the screen. Even Poppy couldn't resist the urge to get up and walk over to get a closer look.

"It looks like a brown blob," she said critically.

"Yes, that's Nessie's head," Oliver said.

Poppy squinted. "Or a close-up of a mushroom," she said.

Oliver Asquith closed his cell phone with a snap. "This photo is going to make history!" he said. "And when the actual video airs—well, it could earn the highest ratings of all my specials. Maybe even the highest TV ratings of all time!"

He gazed around at the Malones and sighed deeply. "Unfortunately, that means that I must leave you," he said. He was trying to sound sorrowful, but he couldn't seem to stop grinning.

"But you just got here!" Franny said in dismay. "And you said you were going to stay for a whole month!"

"Unfortunately, even the best-laid plans must be put aside when history is being made," said Oliver Asquith with a heavy sigh. "I must fly to Scotland immediately to oversee the investigation and make sure that the documentary evidence is preserved."

"Oh no, how disappointing," said Mrs. Malone. "We've barely had any time to visit!"

"Still, I'm sure we'll manage to bear up," said Mr. Malone, who was looking a great deal more cheerful. "Well, you must have a lot to do to get ready for your trip, Oliver, so we'll just head on home, with many thanks for your hospitality and wishing you the best of luck on your travels—"

"Wait." Oliver held up a hand as if he had just been struck by a happy thought. "The network has paid for the houseboat through the end of the month. It seems like a waste to let it sit in the dock, empty. Why don't all of you use it—as my guests, of course?"

"Really?" Will sat up a little straighter. "You mean we can sleep here and use the Jet Skis and everything?"

Oliver Asquith laughed. "You're a few years too young for a Jet Ski," he said. "But you could take out the kayaks if you like, not to mention making full use of the hot tub and the TV—including, of course, the satellite cable—"

"Oh no, Oliver, that's much too generous," Mrs. Malone said, even as her eyes sparkled with delight. "We couldn't *possibly*. . . ."

"Not at all, not at all," said Oliver Asquith, beaming at her. "It is my pleasure. After all, I'm sure you could use the vacation, Emerson. I know it's been stressful for you and Lucille, having such a hard time finding a new case to investigate. . . ."

"Nonsense," Mr. Malone snapped. "It just so happens that there was a newspaper report last week about a UFO that was spotted near Austin. Lucille and I have already started digging into the story. In fact, it's going to take up so much of our time that I'm afraid we'll have to turn down your offer."

"What?" Will said in dismay. "Give up the chance to live on a houseboat for a week?"

"That's so unfair!" Franny said.

"We can research UFOs anytime," Poppy added. "When's the next time we'll be able to spend a week on a lake?"

"I want to stay on the boat," Rolly said. "I want to see the monster."

"For the last time," said Mr. Malone through gritted teeth. "There is no monster!"

"It might be nice to spend some time on the water," said Mrs. Malone wistfully. "The sound of waves is so soothing, isn't it? And so conducive to thinking—"

"I can't believe I'm hearing this!" said Mr. Malone, staring at her. "You've always become violently sick whenever we've had to go to sea. Remember that summer we searched for Atlantis?"

"Only too well," Mrs. Malone said, turning a little green at the memory. "But I only get seasick when I'm actually *at sea*, dear. Lakes are an entirely different matter!"

"Please, Emerson," said Oliver Asquith. "I'd hate to think of all that money that the network spent renting this boat going to waste. It would cheer me up a great deal to think of all of you enjoying yourselves in the sun while I'm trying to stay warm on a cold Scottish lake."

Mr. Malone glared at him. "Thank you," he said stiffly, "but Lucille and I have lots of work to do. Far too much work to spend a whole week sunning ourselves on your boat."

There was a brief, dismayed silence.

Then Mrs. Malone said, in a musing voice, "That's true, dear, we do have work to do. However . . ."

Poppy, Will, and Franny turned to her. When Mrs. Malone used that particular voice, they knew that she had had An Idea. And not just any random, ordinary, run-of-the-mill idea, but An Idea that she herself would have modestly called a "brain wave."

"I've been trying to remember the details of the latest UFO sighting," she went on. "I think . . . I'm almost sure . . . yes, it's coming back to me now! I do believe that the UFO was spotted very near here." She held a hand up to shade her eyes, then pointed toward a road that ran along the lake's edge. "I just read the case file yesterday . . . yes, I think that road over there is the very spot where the witness's car mysteriously stalled!"

She let her voice trail off in a suggestive way.

Poppy, Will, and Franny held their breaths.

"Well," said Mr. Malone meditatively. "It's true that being in the middle of the lake would give us an unobstructed view of the sky."

"And there aren't any streetlights out here," said Will quickly. "No light pollution. Easier to see the aliens."

"It must get really, really, *really* dark at night," Franny chimed in.

"Plus, a lot of UFOs are spotted near water," said Poppy, crossing her fingers. She didn't actually have any evidence of this, but it seemed like a reasonable hypothesis. After all, she thought, seventy percent of the Earth's surface is covered by water, so the odds were in her favor. . . .

Mrs. Malone smiled gently at them. "It's wonderful to see such enthusiasm from all of you when it comes to one of our investigations," she said.

"Yes," agreed Mr. Malone. "And rather peculiar, I might add."

He looked suspiciously at Poppy, Will, and Franny. They did their best to look back with expressions of great sincerity and earnestness.

It must have worked. After a brief pause, Mr. Malone said more briskly, "Still, I'm not one to look a gift horse in the mouth. Given the importance of the work Lucille and I are doing, I think we would be foolish not to accept your offer. Thank you, Oliver. We'll be sure to acknowledge you when our paper is published."

He glanced around at his family's beaming faces. "But remember, we're not staying on this boat to play," he warned them. "We're here to conduct an investigation, and you'll all have to help out."

"We will," said Will.

"We'll do everything you ask us to," said Franny.

"And we'll keep our eyes on the skies at all times," Poppy added. "We promise."

And that, she thought, was a completely safe pledge to make, because there was absolutely nothing weird to see out here on the lake. Nothing at all.

Chapter
THREE

The Malones raced home to pack, then returned to the dock loaded down with duffel bags, telescopes, cameras, DNA testing kits, fishing poles, magnetometers, and a special large box packed with first-aid supplies.

To their delight, they also brought Henry Rivera, their next-door neighbor and now good friend, back with them as well.

"Hey, Franny, do you need some help with that?" Henry asked as Franny wobbled by. She was dragging an oversized suitcase with one hand and holding the handles of two smaller tote bags with the other.

She put the luggage down on the dock with a thump and wiped her forehead. "Thank you,

Henry, that's very nice of you," she said. She turned a scornful look on Will. "It's good to know that *some* boys know how to act like gentlemen."

Will snickered, and Henry's ears turned scarlet.

"I'm not a gentleman," he protested. "I'm a, a . . . what's the opposite of a gentleman?"

"A scoundrel, a bounder, a cad?" suggested Poppy.

"Yes, that's what I am," said Henry. "I'm a cad who happened to notice that Franny's suitcases looked kind of heavy, that's all."

"That's what I mean," said Franny. "You saw someone in need and you offered to help. Unlike some people"—she nodded toward Will—"who simply stand by and let the tired and poor struggle on their own."

"Hey, you pack 'em, you carry 'em," said Will carelessly. "That's my motto. Why do you need all those suitcases anyway? We're just going to be swimming and kayaking."

Franny tossed her head so that her long gold curls flashed in the sun. "That's no reason not to look one's best," she said, surveying Will with a look of distaste. "I'd think you would be ashamed to be seen wearing that outfit."

"It's not an outfit," snapped Will. "It's *clothes*."

He glanced down. His T-shirt told the story of his recent activities (faded ketchup blotches from a food fight with Henry; "Twilight Mist" stains from when he had, under protest, helped Mrs. Malone paint the front porch; dirt and grass stains from an ambitious attempt to build a tunnel from the house to the tool-shed; and several rips from the day he climbed the tallest oak tree in the woods). His khaki shorts had also suffered in these adventures, plus he had now worn them for a record seven days in a row.

"And anyway," he said, "what's wrong with what I'm wearing?"

She raised one eyebrow. "If I didn't know any better, I'd think you just came back from five months in the wilderness."

"Awesome," he said stoutly. "That's exactly the look I was going for."

Franny rolled her eyes. "Just promise you'll

stay far away from me. I'd like to make some new friends, thank you very much, and I don't want them scared off by my little brother."

"No problem," said Will. "I'll get started right now. Come on, Henry. Let's move far, far away and get the magnetometer out of the car."

As the boys moved away, Poppy asked Franny, "Who do you think you're going to meet in the middle of the lake?"

As if in answer to her question, a boy with white-blond hair sped past on a Jet Ski, leaving a ripple of water in his wake. He was moving fast, but he still managed to flash a smile in their direction. Franny tucked a strand of hair behind her ear and smiled back.

"Oh," said Poppy. "Right."

Franny tossed her head. "You don't need to sneer," she said. "What's wrong with making new friends?"

Nothing, Poppy thought. The problem is that we never stay anywhere long enough for them to become *old* friends.

"We don't need to make any new friends," said Poppy. "We have Henry."

"Henry is nice," Franny admitted, "but he's just one person."

"One is enough," said Poppy. "If it's the right person."

"That's what you think now," Franny said darkly. "But you feel differently when you get to be my age."

She put on a quoting voice. "A young person needs at least three close friends who will offer support and a listening ear in order to make it through the stresses and traumas of middle school." She paused long enough to give Poppy a significant look. "And I'm going to be in a brand-new middle school! That means I'll have twice the trauma! I'll probably need a half dozen good friends just to make it to high school without suffering serious psychological damage!"

Mrs. Malone, clutching a telescope and tripod in her arms, staggered past just in time to hear the end of this.

"You're not still going on about middle school trauma, are you?" said Mrs. Malone, giving her a harassed look. "Honestly, Franny, going from sixth to seventh grade is not quite the same as climbing Qomolangma in search of Yeti. Poppy, where did you put the night-vision goggles? I can't find them anywhere."

"They're in the trunk of the car," said Poppy. "Hold on, I'll get them."

As she ran down the gangplank, she passed Mr. Malone, who was carrying a stack of books about the Roswell UFO crash.

"Watch out!" gasped Mr. Malone, whose armful of books tilted precariously as Poppy ran past.

"I can take some of those, Mr. Malone," said Henry.

"That's all right, I've got it," gasped Mr. Malone. The top book slipped. Mr. Malone reached up to grab it, which disturbed the balance of the whole pile. A half dozen books began tilting, as if in slow motion.

"Drat!" said Mr. Malone as he backpedaled, trying to keep the books balanced. At the last possible moment, just as he was about to step backward off the gangplank and fall into the lake, Henry neatly lifted the top of the stack from Mr. Malone's arms, allowing Mr. Malone to regain his own balance.

"Thank you, Henry," he gasped. "Of course, I had everything under control, but still . . . thank you."

"Would you cut it out, Henry?" said Will from the side of his mouth. "You're going to make me look bad."

Once they got all their gear stowed and clothes put away, the Malones gathered on the deck.

"What should we do first?" asked Will. "Go swimming? Try the waterslide? Take out the kayaks?"

"The answer is none of the above," said Mr. Malone. "Not until you all help me put this up on the outside of the cabin."

Poppy, Will, and Franny turned to see Mr. Malone unrolling a long, unwieldy canvas that he had carted from home.

"Don't just stand there gaping!" he called out. "Come over here and lend a hand."

Dragging their feet, they walked over to where

the canvas, now unrolled, was covering a large section of the deck.

The dark blue canvas was twenty feet square and covered with line drawings of aliens. Some had large heads and narrow eyes, some were squat and dumpy, some were tall and thin, some had eight long, thin fingers on each hand and some had tentacles. Various types of spacecraft—flying saucers, strange trapezoid shapes and what looked like dirigibles—were drawn around the border.

"What," asked Franny, "is *that*?"

"A present from Wilbur," said Mr. Malone. He stood up, beads of sweat rolling down his face. He took off his glasses and wiped them on his T-shirt, blinking nearsightedly. "It arrived yesterday from Berlin."

"That explains a lot," muttered Will.

Professor Wilbur Sutterwaite had spent his long and controversial career studying UFOs. Mr. Malone had taken a seminar course from the professor as part of his junior year abroad and they had stayed in touch ever since, exchanging chatty letters filled with news about their families, crop circles, career moves, mysterious ship disappearances, travel plans, and famous unsolved UFO sightings.

"Of course, we should have known," said Will. "Is he still collecting stories about those green glowing spheres that keep floating around the sky in Argentina?"

Mrs. Malone clucked her tongue in exasperation. "I do wish you children would pay a little more attention to dinner table conversation, instead of making mashed potato forts and pelting them with peas," she said. "I know I told you all about how he had to flee South America after that unfortunate misunderstanding—"

"You mean when he hiked up a mountain and found that little cave?" asked Poppy.

"The cave that he camped out in?" added Will. "The one that turned out to be a sacred temple of the moon?"

"And then had to run back down the mountain to escape from an angry mob?" finished Franny.

"That unfortunate misunderstanding?" asked Poppy, driving the point home.

"All right," Mrs. Malone said testily. "I see I was wrong. Apparently, you *do* pay attention. Although I don't see what you all think is so funny. The poor man was a nervous wreck for six months."

"At any rate, he's moved on," said Mr. Malone. "He's investigating crop circles now. He's come up with some very interesting data. Did you know that electronic equipment often fails when it's taken near a crop circle?"

"Maybe that explains why none of the people who claim they've seen a crop circle appear right before their eyes have actually managed to film it," murmured Poppy.

"Eyewitness accounts are just as good," said Mr. Malone. "In fact, that was Wilbur's inspiration for this poster. He hired a police sketch artist to take all those descriptions of aliens and their spacecraft and make drawings of them. And this is the result!"

He waved a hand proudly at the poster.

Franny stared at it in disgust. "That is probably the single most uncool thing I have ever seen," she said. "And that is saying a lot, considering that I have spent the first thirteen years of my life in this family. Please please *please* don't tell me you're actually going to hang that up. Everybody who comes within a hundred yards of our boat will see it!"

"Exactly! That was your father's idea, and it was an absolute brainstorm," said Mrs. Malone happily. "You see, the more people who notice the poster, the more awareness we will raise about the possibility of alien visitations. And the more people who are watching for aliens, the more sightings we're likely to get."

"Don't worry," Poppy said to Franny. "At least nobody will be able to see it at night."

"But that's the best part," said Mrs. Malone with delight. "It was painted with phosphorescent paint! That means—"

"It glows in the dark," Poppy said to Franny.

Franny sighed. "Of course it does."

* * *

Half an hour later, they had finally hung the poster. Poppy held up one corner and Henry the other, while Mrs. Malone and Will stood back saying things like, "It's tilted a little to the left . . . try straightening it a bit . . . that's it . . . no, now it's tilting to the right. . . ." and Mr. Malone managed to hit his thumb a half dozen times while trying to hammer nails into the wood. Everybody had lost their tempers at least once but, in the end, the deed was done.

Then Mrs. Malone pulled out her file of local UFO sightings and suggested that they cruise over to where a UFO had most recently been seen and drop anchor for the night. Mr. Malone stepped to the bridge and confidently flipped a switch to start the engine.

The engine turned over. He smiled and put the engine in gear—and then it sputtered and died.

He tried again.

Again, the engine turned over for a few seconds, then gasped to a halt.

"Darling, perhaps I should try," suggested Mrs. Malone.

"No, no, I've got this," said Mr. Malone, waving her off. "There's a certain knack to starting these things up, you know."

Frowning, he fiddled with the key. As he did so, another houseboat chugged past them, stopping a few yards away. A girl about Franny's age stood at the railing, while a boy who looked a little older sat in a deck chair. They were clearly brother and sister—both had blond hair so pale that it looked almost white. The girl was examining the Malones with cheerful interest, but the boy stared off into the distance as if he hadn't even noticed they were there.

A man wearing white shorts and a blue-flowered Hawaiian shirt came out of the cabin and called out, "Ahoy there! Is this your first time on the water?"

"Not at all," said Mr. Malone irritably. "In fact, I once steered a longboat canoe down a Bolivian river in search of El Ucumar—"

He tried again. The engine stalled.

His shoulders slumped in defeat. "Of course,

that was some time ago," he admitted.

"And remember, dear, we had six young men helping us row," said Mrs. Malone. She waved cheerfully at the man. "We'd be glad of some help!"

The man stepped from his boat to the Malones' and introduced himself. "Charley Cameron," he said. "And this is my daughter, Ashley, and my son, Colt."

"Hi!" Ashley called out with a cheerful smile, but Colt merely waved a lazy hello from where he was sitting in a deck chair, then closed his eyes as if he were about to take a nap.

Ashley rolled her eyes. "*Colt* is too good to come over and talk to us," she said. "*Colt* is going to be a freshman in high school this fall. And *Colt*"—she grinned and jumped across the gap between the two boats—"doesn't lower himself by talking to people who are only going to be in seventh grade."

"Me, too!" Franny said with delight. "I mean, I'll be in the seventh grade, too."

"Which school?"

"McCallum."

"That's where I'm going in the fall!"

And with that, Franny and Ashley retreated to the stern of the boat to huddle, their heads together, and talk about the mysteries that awaited them in middle school.

Mr. Cameron rocked back on his heels and squinted up at the poster of alien sketches.

"That's a right interesting decoration you got there," he said. "You're interested in little green men, I take it?"

"We are not just interested in them," said Mrs. Malone proudly. "We study them. You see, we are paranormal investigators—"

"Oh yeah, like that other fellow who was out here on your boat," the man said. "That Oliver Asquith fellow who's on TV all the time. You friends of his?"

Mr. Malone's smile seemed to freeze. "In a manner of speaking," he said in measured tones. "He is one of our colleagues—"

"Oh, he's more than that, Emerson!" trilled Mrs. Malone. She said confidingly to Mr. Cameron,

"He's actually a very close family friend. In fact, he's Franny's godfather."

"That right?" Mr. Cameron said. "I heard he was going to film one of his TV shows here. Something about a lake monster."

"Yes," Mr. Malone said coolly.

"Do you like Dr. Asquith's work?" asked Mrs. Malone. "It's too bad he's gone. He loves to meet his fans."

Mr. Cameron shrugged. "Well now, I don't know that I'd say I was a *fan*, exactly," he said. "His show's interesting but I think he was barking up the wrong tree when he came to Austin. This lake's never had a monster that I heard of, and I've lived here all my life."

Mr. Malone perked up. "Exactly as I thought! Oliver has a tendency to believe every half-baked story he hears." He shook his head sadly. "It's a terrible thing to be so gullible, especially when one claims to be a scientist—"

"Now, Emerson," said Mrs. Malone sternly. "Perhaps Oliver is a little more open-minded than the rest of us, but he does have a track record of investigating strange stories and finding that there's some truth behind them."

"The only story I ever heard around these parts was about Mugwump," said Mr. Cameron. "Now there have been plenty of sightings of that old fellow. In fact, one of my buddies saw him, oh, let's see"—he squinted as if trying to remember—"just about a year ago."

"Really?" Mrs. Malone cast a triumphant look at her husband. "So Oliver was right! There *is* a monster here."

"Well, no," said Mr. Cameron. "Not unless you count a big ol' catfish. And *mean*! I wouldn't want to hook that ol' Mugwump, I tell you what."

Mr. Malone snorted. "An overfed catfish? That hardly ranks with the Loch Ness monster."

"You don't know that, Emerson," said Mrs. Malone. "After all, we haven't seen this creature. Perhaps it's some kind of mutant!"

Mr. Cameron shrugged. "Could be, I guess. But that's not the strangest thing I've seen out here.

Now, if you wanted to look into some seriously weird stuff, I could tell you things—"

"Where is Mugwump?" asked Rolly. "I want to see him."

Mr. Cameron chuckled. "Why's that?" he asked. "You want to catch him?"

Rolly's eyes narrowed. After some thought, he said, "Yes. I do."

He said that in the firm and resolute voice that made every other Malone shiver.

"Stop right there," said Mr. Malone. "You are not—I repeat, *not*—going to try to catch this Mugglegump."

"Mugwump," said Mr. Cameron.

Mr. Malone swept on. "The last thing we need is a gigantic catfish with a bad temper flopping around on the deck," hc said.

Rolly gave him a black look and headed for the wheelhouse.

"Er . . . exactly how big is this Wumgum supposed to be?" asked Mrs. Malone as she nervously kept one eye on Rolly.

"Mugwump," corrected Mr. Cameron. "My buddy said maybe five feet long, and near on fifty pounds. 'Course, he's a little prone to exaggeration. I remember one time he said he saw a possum that was as big as a polecat. Well, it turns out that possum was actually about the size of my wife's miniature poodle—"

"Mom!" Rolly trotted back, carrying a fishing pole. "I need some bait."

Mrs. Malone gave Rolly a stern glance. "You are not going to try to catch this Wugmup," she said firmly.

"Mugwump," Rolly said absently.

"I don't care what his name is!" Mrs. Malone said. "Something that big could drag you right off the boat! It's far too dangerous."

Rolly turned to Mr. Cameron. "What does a monster catfish like to eat?"

"Well, worms wouldn't be more than a nibble to a monster like that," Mr. Cameron said. "Maybe you could try a raw chicken, if your mom would let you have one instead of cooking it for dinner."

He winked at Mrs. Malone in a way that showed he wasn't taking Rolly's new ambition very seriously.

The rest of the Malones—who knew only too well where Rolly's obsessions could lead—were.

"Rolly. You are *not* going to try to catch that fish," said Mrs. Malone in measured tones. "I absolutely forbid it."

But Rolly was not listening. His gaze had locked onto a box of donuts that Mr. Malone had brought on deck to keep Poppy, Franny, and Will from grumbling too much as they helped hang up the alien poster. The box was open. Only half a donut and a few crumbs were left. Rolly grabbed the piece of donut, stuck it on his fishhook, then dropped the line over the railing.

"Rolly, I said—" warned Mrs. Malone.

"Oh, I wouldn't worry too much about the boy if I were you," said Mr. Cameron easily. "People have been fishing in this lake for years, and no one's got so much as a nibble. Now, if you wanted to look into some seriously weird stuff, I could tell you a few things. Take those little buggers right there." He nodded at the alien spotting poster. "I'm here to tell you, those things are real," said Mr. Cameron. "You know how I know? 'Cause I've seen 'em."

"You have?" Mr. Malone sounded friendlier. "Where? When?"

"Right here on this lake." Mr. Cameron waved expansively at the water. "I've seen weird lights in the sky, oh, maybe half a dozen times. Lights that zip back and forth too fast to be an airplane, you know what I mean?"

"Of course! That's one of the classic signs of a UFO," said Mrs. Malone. She pulled her shopping list out of her one pocket and a pencil stub from the other and began scribbling notes. "Tell me, did you notice any problems with your electrical equipment? Or maybe you experienced a strange loss of time—"

"Hey, you know what I read in *The Rational Scientist* last month?" Poppy said. "There was an article about a study of UFO encounters. The woman who did the study interviewed people who had seen UFOs. You know what she found out? Nine out of ten people who saw UFOs said that they had really, *really* wanted to see a UFO. Doesn't that seem like quite a coincidence?"

Mr. Cameron held up his hands in protest. "Hey, I never wanted to get anywhere near one of those things," he said. "I've heard stories, you know. They might just beam me up and shoot off to another galaxy. Now that would not suit me—I'm just too much of a homebody—but as I understand it the little green men don't give you much of a say in the matter—"

"Did you report your sighting to anyone?" asked Mrs. Malone. "Was there an investigation?"

"Of course I did! And would you believe, the Austin Police Department, the Texas Rangers, and the United States Air Force all told me that I was seeing things?" He shook his head in disgust. "They must think I just fell off the turnip truck."

"Where did these sightings take place?" asked Mrs. Malone. Her glasses had slipped down her nose. She peered over the lenses at Mr. Cameron.

"Can you show us the spot?"

"Sure. It was right over there, Cowart's Cove," he said, pointing to the far side of the lake. "I'd be glad to take y'all over there and tell you the whole dang story."

"That would be wonderful." Mrs. Malone turned to Mr. Malone, beaming. "Emerson, dear, we must calibrate the AlienScope immediately! It would be awful if UFOs suddenly appeared and we weren't ready."

"You're absolutely right, my dear, as always." Mr. Malone rubbed his hands together briskly. "Now, let's see . . . Poppy, you're the best person to take charge of the calibration, of course. Will, why don't you set up the spectrometer and show Henry how to use it to scan the skies. I think you two can take first watch tonight. And Franny—"

"I can't," said Franny quickly. "Ashley invited me to go on their boat." She gave Mrs. Malone a pleading look. "You have to let me go. She's telling me all about middle school. It will help me with the trauma of transition."

Ashley opened her eyes wide and nodded vigorously. "It's a stressful time for a preadolescent," she said. "I'd be glad to help Franny orient herself to a new school environment in order to ensure that she has the best academic and social experience possible. After all, if she doesn't receive the support and encouragement she needs, the experience could end up"—Ashley whispered the last words—"damaging her self-esteem."

Mrs. Malone took a deep breath. "Thank you, Ashley, but I think Franny's self-esteem is strong enough to survive on its own," she said evenly. "At a moment like this, everyone in the family has to—"

"Pitch in," Franny interrupted. "Of course. You're absolutely right, Mother."

Mrs. Malone's mouth hung open slightly in surprise.

Poppy caught Will's eye and raised one eyebrow.

"Something's up," she whispered. Will nodded.

"And I *do* want to help out," said Franny earnestly.

"Wait for it," muttered Poppy.

"I really do." Franny widened her eyes. "In fact, I have an awesome idea!"

"Brace yourself," said Will.

"I'd like to interview Mr. Cameron about the time he saw a UFO," Franny finished smoothly. "It would be good to have a transcript for our records, wouldn't it?"

Poppy and Will looked at each other in astonishment. Franny was right. That was a brilliant idea—at least, it was a brilliant idea for getting to spend time with Ashley, on the Camerons' houseboat, far away from Mr. and Mrs. Malone's doomed attempts to spot UFOs.

"Yes! You are absolutely correct!" cried Mr. Malone, pointing to Franny as if she'd just offered the winning answer on a TV game show. "Excellent plan, Franny. Take one of the tape recorders from the equipment trunk and a copy of our standard Paranormal Event Witness Questionnaire. And don't forget to ask Mr. Cameron to make sketches of what he saw."

"I won't, Dad! Thanks!" With a triumphant

flip of her hair, Franny ran below to grab a tote bag from her berth.

Will watched her go. "Okay," he said to Poppy. "I'm officially impressed. Franny always seems like such a ditz—then once in a while, she pulls off something clever like that. It's enough to make you wonder if it's all just an act."

"You mean, maybe she's secretly brilliant but she's hiding it from us?" Poppy asked.

"Yeah." His eyes slid sideways to meet hers. They grinned at each other.

"Nah," they said together.

It had been, as Mrs. Malone said, a long day. That was her excuse for making everyone go to bed early. Poppy knew this really meant that Mrs. Malone desperately wanted to go to sleep, but for once she didn't mind. The combination of unpacking their gear and the heat of the day had made her tired.

The houseboat had several bedrooms. Mr. and Mrs. Malone had one, of course (with Rolly safely tucked into a small bed in the corner, where they could keep an eye on him). Henry and Will were sharing the other large bedroom. Poppy and Franny each got their own tiny room that had a small window and a single bunk with two drawers for clothing tucked under the bed. Franny muttered a bit about the lack of space, but Poppy was delighted. When she put on her pajamas and got into bed, she felt as snug as a turtle in its shell.

Yawning, she turned out the light, then turned on her side to look out the window. A new moon floated in the dark sky. She could just see the silhouettes of a few other boats anchored some distance away, and the faint moonlight reflecting off the water's ripples.

She felt her eyes closing. Before I know it, it will be tomorrow, she thought sleepily. The first day of a whole week on the lake . . .

She yawned again and punched up her pillow.

Then something—later, she could never say what—made her open her eyes one more time before falling asleep.

That was when she saw the lights dancing along the distant shore. She blinked. She squeezed her eyes shut and opened them again. The lights looked like fireflies, although of course they couldn't be. There was no way she could see fireflies from this far away.

But they flickered through the air like fireflies, randomly darting this way and that, tiny trails of cold green light. At least . . . she narrowed her eyes, trying to watch carefully. At least the movement of the lights *seemed* to be random at first. But the more she watched, the more she realized that there was pattern to what she was seeing. A pattern . . . almost like a dance.

They're just lights from a campout someone is having on shore, she told herself.

Then she remembered how she had (most sensibly) researched Lake Travis's water recreation and safety rules the night before.

She had learned that life jackets were required when kayaking, that anyone who threw trash in the lake would be fined—and that no campfires were allowed on shore, due to a drought that had lasted for three months.

She stared harder at the lights—and at that moment, they suddenly arced into the air in unison, fell toward the water, and disappeared.

Poppy blinked, then flopped down on her berth and gazed out the small porthole. The moon had risen and was floating, round and glowing, in the dark sky. The sight of moonlight—a perfectly natural and explainable source of light—comforted her. There was something a little spooky about those green lights and the way they seemed to follow each other around. . . .

A chill shivered along her spine. Irritably, Poppy shook herself, then thumped her pillow a few times and laid back down.

This is ridiculous, she told herself sternly. You're as bad as someone who screams at those silly ghost stories people tell at camp. You probably just imagined the lights. Or maybe your eyes were playing tricks on you. . . .

Then her mind went back to all the weird things

that had happened since they had moved to Austin. She had thought she was seeing things when that goblin appeared in the attic, and the next thing she knew, Rolly had been replaced with a changeling and she had had to lead an expedition into a goblin cave to rescue him. And she had thought she was imagining things when she saw that stone angel at the cemetery smirking down at her, and the next thing she knew, their house was haunted by not just one, but six ghosts (to say nothing of the phantom dog).

Still, what were the odds that she was about to have yet another paranormal adventure?

"There's got to be a reasonable explanation for those lights," she whispered to herself as she finally closed her eyes. "After all, weird things don't happen in threes, not really. . . ."

Chapter
FOUR

Poppy was awakened the next morning by the sound of her mother shouting.

"Rolly, watch it—*aggh*!" Mrs. Malone yelled.

In a flash, Poppy pulled on her T-shirt and shorts and raced up to the deck, where she saw Mrs. Malone clutching her head and leaning over in a most peculiar way. Rolly stood some distance away, holding an old fishing pole that Mr. Malone had bought in a flurry of enthusiasm and that had gathered dust in every attic of every house they lived in ever since.

"What's wrong?" asked Poppy.

"Rolly is still trying to catch that silly lake monster," Mrs. Malone said through gritted teeth. "The problem is that the only thing he's caught is *me*."

Poppy looked more closely and saw that a fishing lure was tangled in Mrs. Malone's hair.

"Hold still. I think I can get it out," Poppy said, reaching forward to unsnag the lure.

"Ouch!" cried Mrs. Malone.

"Sorry." Poppy glared at Rolly. "What did you think you were *doing*?"

"Practicing," said Rolly. "First, I have to practice casting. That's when you put the hook in the water. Then I have to practice pulling the fish in." He lifted the pole experimentally and began to wind the reel.

"Don't!" cried out Mrs. Malone, putting both hands on her head and stumbling toward him. "I am not a fish!"

"I know," said Rolly. "But Mr. Cameron said Ol' Mugwump is huge. He's as big as a whale." He gave Mrs. Malone a measuring look. "I think you'll be good practice."

Mrs. Malone stopped in her tracks. Poppy took advantage of this to yank the lure out, not bothering to be gentle, and Mrs. Malone strode forward to snatch the fishing pole out of Rolly's hands.

"Excuse me," she said in an awful voice. "I'm sure I must have misheard you, Rolly. I'm sure you didn't say that I look like a whale!"

"No, of course I didn't," said Rolly. "I wouldn't say that." He sounded so honestly puzzled that Mrs. Malone relaxed a little.

"Well, good—" she began.

"Whales have waterspouts on the top of their heads," he pointed out. "You don't have a waterspout. And whales don't wear clothes. Or dye their hair—"

"I do not dye my hair!" shouted Mrs. Malone. "Honestly, sometimes I don't have a clue how your mind works."

Poppy raised her eyebrows. Mrs. Malone was usually the one member of the family who always took Rolly's side. When he wrote with a black marker all over a freshly painted wall, it was a sign of artistic genius. When he climbed on the roof and methodically threw three dozen eggs to the ground, it was a sign of scientific curiosity. When he took every pillow in the house to the backyard, made a giant pile, and almost jumped off the porch roof (Poppy had grabbed him just in time), it was a sign of innovation, risk taking, and creative thinking.

But getting a fishing lure caught in her hair and being compared to a whale seemed to have been the last straw.

"I told you it was a bad idea to give Rolly a fishing pole," Poppy pointed out.

"Yes, well, thank you for that advice," Mrs. Malone said tartly. "Of course, it's always easy to see what will happen *after* the fact—"

Poppy decided not to point out that she had warned her mother before the fact. When someone has been caught with a fishing lure and called a whale and revealed as a person who possibly dyed her hair—well, in Poppy's opinion, that person had already suffered quite enough.

When Poppy finally made her way over to where two kayaks were hung on the side of the boat, she found that Will and Henry had already put on their life jackets and were taking down one of the kayaks.

"Kayaking's not hard at all," Will was saying. "Not once you get the hang of it, anyway."

"Oh, yeah?" said Henry, panting a little as he helped Will lower the kayak to the deck. "I tried canoeing once at summer camp and I just kept going around in circles."

"Will and I can teach you," Poppy said, grabbing a life jacket for herself. "We learned two summers ago, when Mom and Dad were trying to track down the Everglades Skunk Ape."

Henry's eyes brightened. "Really? I've never heard of a skunk ape. Did you actually see one?"

"Nope," said Will. "But we did have a close encounter with the Everglades Monster Snake—"

"For the last time, nothing was pulling you down to the bottom of the swamp," said Poppy. "You just got a vine wrapped around your foot."

"It was a Monster Snake," said Will stubbornly. "Not only that, it was a Monster Snake with bad intentions. It would have drowned me if I hadn't managed to wrest free of its evil grasp."

Poppy winked at Henry. "You just keep telling that story, Will," she said. "That's what you're good at."

Then she looked at the kayak they were about to launch. Will and Henry had taken down a double, which left another double and a single kayak.

"We're taking a double, so I can teach Henry how to kayak. You can take the single, Poppy," Will said briskly. He nodded to Henry. "Come on, let's lower it over the side—"

Poppy's smile dimmed and she felt her spirits droop a little. Instantly, she told herself she was being silly. After all, she *liked* exploring on her own. And she knew from experience how bossy Will could get when he was trying to steer anything (kayak, canoe, paddleboat, or bumper car) with another person. She certainly wasn't looking forward to kayaking with him again.

Still, she thought, I could have taken the double with Henry. That would have worked just as well. . . .

"Or I could go with Henry and you could take the single kayak," Poppy said casually. "I think that would be more fun for Henry. You always get mad when someone else is in your kayak. You always start shouting."

Will glared at her. "Only when certain people collide with a submerged log."

"You said to paddle harder," Poppy snapped. "So I did."

"Yes, I remember," he snapped back. "Which is why we rammed into a log at the speed of sound, which is why we tipped over, which is how I ended up being pulled underwater by the Everglades Monster Snake—"

"Got your foot tangled by a vine," Poppy said under her breath.

"And almost drowned," Will finished.

Poppy opened her mouth to argue, but before she could say anything, Will grabbed the front of the double kayak. "Henry, you take the back and help me lower it over the side."

Henry glanced at Poppy and gave an apologetic

little shrug. "We can go out next time," he said. "Once I get the hang of this."

"Sure," she said, trying to sound as if it didn't matter to her one way or the other. "Then I can just correct everything Will's taught you."

Henry grinned, jumped up on the railing, and launched himself into the air, landing in the water with a huge splash. Will followed him, leaving Poppy to get her kayak down by herself. By the time she was paddling away from the houseboat, Henry and Will were already more than a dozen yards away.

"This is the forward stroke," she could hear Will saying. "See, like this." He demonstrated.

"Got it," said Henry, copying Will's movement perfectly.

"And this is the sweep stroke," said Will.

"Got it."

"And this," added Will with a grin, "is the tip-over stroke."

With that, he suddenly reached with his paddle, leaning out so far that the kayak rolled over in the water. A few seconds later, Will and Henry both came to the surface, spluttering.

"You just learned your first lesson, Henry," Poppy said.

"How to get out of an overturned kayak?" he asked.

"No," she said. "How you should never trust Will."

"Everyone tips over sooner or later," said Will, treading water, his eyes dancing with mischief. "I just wanted to get it out of the way. Now we won't be waiting and wondering about when it's going to happen."

"Well, I'm going to paddle to the shoreline if you want to come along," Poppy said. "I brought some specimen jars and my microscope with me. I thought I'd collect some water samples for analysis—"

"Stop, stop." Will held a hand to his head as if he were about to faint. "I think I'm going to pass out from all the excitement."

Henry laughed. It was just a small laugh, but

Poppy felt hurt all the same.

"I happen to think that's interesting," she said coolly.

"Sorry, Poppy," said Henry, but he was biting his lip not to smile. "We weren't making fun of you, really. It's just that collecting water samples on vacation is such a . . . well, such a *Poppy* thing to do."

"If you're going to do a science project, why not look for Ol' Mugwump?" asked Will. "At least finding a giant catfish would be cool. Algae is just lame."

"It would also be a waste of time," she snapped. "You know that Oliver Asquith makes all that stuff up for his TV shows."

"I think Poppy's right," said Henry. "I've lived in Austin all my life. There's nothing spooky or weird in this lake. I would have heard about it."

"But a monster sounds more exciting," said Will. "It sounds more fun. . . ."

They continued to argue in a friendly way as Will showed Henry how to get back into a kayak, a maneuver that took more time—and involved more splashing and yelling—than Poppy would have thought possible.

As she waited, her thoughts drifted.

The water was so calm today, she thought. People always compare calm water to a mirror, and today she could see why. She leaned over slightly to look at her reflection. . . .

Out of the corner of her eye, Poppy saw a shining, spangled scaly thing slide under her kayak. She jerked upright again.

"Hey, what was that?" she asked.

"What was what?" Henry panted as he tried to get his legs back into the kayak.

She leaned over, peering into the water, but whatever she saw—or thought she saw—had vanished.

"I thought I saw something swim under my kayak," she said. "It looked like a fish."

"No kidding," said Will, deadpan. "That's incredible. I mean here we are, on a lake, and you see a fish in the water. Amazing."

"It looked like a big fish," said Poppy, ignoring his sarcasm. She squinted against the sun and tilted her head, first to the right, then to the left, hoping to get another glimpse. "Really big. Enormous."

"Maybe you spotted Ol' Mugwump," said Will.

"No such thing," she said automatically, not bothering to look up.

"It could have been a catfish," suggested Henry. "Some of them can get pretty big."

"It didn't look like a catfish," she said, remembering that flash of blue and silver, that supple, curving movement.

Henry grinned. "What—can you identify different species of fish on sight?"

Will rolled his eyes. "Do you really have to ask?"

Henry's grin widened, and Poppy felt herself blush.

"When I found out we were moving to Austin, naturally I started researching the flora and the fauna of the area—" she said stiffly.

"Naturally," Henry said, biting his lip to hide his smile.

"Okay, so it wasn't a catfish," said Will. "And it wasn't Mugwump the Monster. So what was it?"

"I'm not sure," said Poppy slowly. "It didn't look like any of the photos I've studied. It almost didn't look like a fish at all. It looked too . . . I don't know . . . elegant."

"Elegant!" The boys hooted.

Poppy felt her face heat up. "Yes," she said. "Elegant. And you can laugh, but *I* saw it. You didn't."

"It would be better if it was monstrous and horrible looking," said Will. "Then we could sell your story to one of those supermarket newspapers that like weird stories. You know"—he put on a deep voice—"'A Mutant from the Deep!'"

"'The Loathsome Leviathan!'" added Henry.

"'The Lake Travis Travesty!'" said Will.

Poppy's kayak rocked as something— something large and powerful—moved under her.

"There!" she said, twisting in her seat to peer into the water. "Didn't you feel that?"

Will said, "Nope. Not a thing—"

Poppy saw his eyes widen with surprise as his kayak pitched up and down. In the next instant, the swell of water had reached her.

She heard Henry yell, "Whoa!"

She saw Will lose his grip on his paddle.

And before she could take a breath, her kayak flipped over and she found herself upside down in the water.

Poppy opened her eyes automatically, even as she pulled her legs from the kayak and swam toward the surface. She couldn't see much of anything.

But somehow, even through the water drumming in her ears, she thought she heard something. . . .

Before she could figure out what it was, she reached the surface. Her head popped above the water, and she took in a deep breath.

A few feet away, Henry and Will were treading water next to their overturned kayak.

"What happened?" Henry asked.

Will blinked water out of his eyes. "It was that

speedboat," he said, glaring after a sleek white blur that was already disappearing into the distance. "It went by so fast, the wake flipped us over."

Poppy grabbed her kayak before it could float away, then swam closer to them. "The wake wasn't that strong," she said. "And the speedboat wasn't that close."

Henry looked puzzled. "But what else could have tipped us over?"

She hesitated, wondering whether to say anything. Will and Henry would probably laugh at her. They would probably turn whatever she said into a joke. They would probably tease her for days. And yet . . .

A good scientist, she reminded herself, always tries to confirm her observations.

"Did you, well, hear anything?" she asked. "When you were underwater?"

"I wasn't listening; I was trying not to drown," Will said, rather grumpily. Once again, he and Henry were clambering back into their kayak. Will did not seem to find this exercise as appealing the second time around.

"Come on," he said to Henry. "Let's see how fast we can get to that fallen oak tree over there."

They shot off for the distant shore, the spray from their paddles glittering in the sun.

Poppy watched them go, trying not to feel as if she'd been left behind on purpose. Trying not to feel left behind, left alone, left out.

The only sounds were the lapping of the water against her kayak and the distant sound of laughter from the Camerons' houseboat.

But Poppy knew what she had heard—a faint chiming sound, as if bells were ringing under the lake.

If she didn't know better, she would have said the bells sounded eerily like laughter. . . .

Chapter
FIVE

That's okay, Poppy was telling herself a couple of hours later. I'm *glad* I have a kayak to myself. I'm *glad* Will and Henry went off without me. I'm *glad* I'm on my own. Now I can go off to collect lake water without having anyone making fun of me.

None of this was exactly the truth, but she repeated it over and over to herself as she began paddling. By the time she got to the small cove, she almost believed it.

It was farther away than it had looked on the map. By the time she got there, she was hot and sweaty. She paddled along a small creek that led to the cove. There were trees overhanging the creek, providing welcome shade. Poppy took a drink from her water bottle and paddled along more slowly, watching the fish and turtles in the water, listening to the birds in the trees, and, without noticing it, getting farther and farther from any of the boats on the lake.

The creek widened and the cove, a small inlet of water, lay before her. Poppy gently paddled into the middle of the inlet, then pulled her paddle from the water and laid it across the kayak.

For a few moments, she enjoyed just sitting still as her kayak rocked gently on the water. She tilted her head back to look at the cloudless blue sky and realized with surprise that the sun was beginning to set. She had been out longer than she thought. The sky directly above her was still pale blue and filled with light. But the shadows had begun to creep from under the trees, and near the horizon the sky was turning a deep blue.

She glanced back at the houseboat, then looked at her watch. It had taken her almost two hours to get here, but then she had stopped often to fill a tiny bottle with water or to watch a turtle sunning itself on a rock. She could probably make it back to the houseboat in time for dinner, although she would be scolded for being out too long.

If anyone even misses me, she thought, a trifle bitterly.

Franny would be too busy with her new friend Ashley to spare anyone else a thought. Rolly would be focused on his pursuit of the lake monster. Mr. and Mrs. Malone would be deeply involved in their latest investigation. And Will and Henry . . .

Poppy scowled ferociously.

How long, she wondered, would it take for them to realize she wasn't with them? How long would it take for them to get worried?

She glared at the houseboat, then turned her back on it, picking up her paddle.

If no one cares about where I am, she thought, straightening her shoulders, then I might as well see what's around that next bend.

As she began navigating her way through the narrow channel, she took a deep breath. The air smelled like cedar, wildflowers, and . . . wood smoke?

But no one's allowed to build fires on the shore, she thought, just as she reached the bend in the creek. With two swift paddle strokes, she had turned the kayak and found herself gliding onto a large pool of water.

On the right side of the pool, there was a clearing ringed with oak trees. In the middle of the clearing, a small bonfire was burning merrily.

And around the bonfire were three girls, dancing.

Poppy performed a backward power stroke to stop her kayak from moving closer to the shore. She waited in the shadows, just outside of the ring of light cast by the bonfire, and watched.

The figures were moving around the fire in a circle. Two of the girls looked like teenagers and one girl looked close to Poppy's age. An older woman with silver hair that fell to her waist sat nearby, on a log, playing what looked like a small harp and singing.

The dance didn't look formal. It almost seemed that they were drifting around the fire aimlessly.

But the more she watched, the more Poppy noticed that there seemed to be a pattern to the dance, although she couldn't quite figure out what it was. The figures would weave in and out, first blocking the fire so that they were dark shapes against the blaze, then moving on so that the flames blazed brightly against the dark woods.

Poppy blinked, frustrated that when she thought she had grasped what the pattern was, the figures would move again and the meaning of it would escape her.

The music was just as maddening. There didn't seem to be a tune, just a wavering melody that went up and down. And yet, every once in a while, a few notes would seem to resolve themselves into something that sounded like a song . . . and then the next instant it would be lost again.

Poppy let her gaze slip past the dancers to see if she could spot some clue to who they were and what they were doing there.

Not that it was really any of her business, of

course. It was just that the scene seemed so odd, so out of place.

She remembered some of the bedtime stories Mrs. Malone used to tell them when they were small, in the fond belief that they would find them soothing and would fall asleep more quickly. Stories about fairy rings and the Other Folk who would steal babies from the cradle or lure grown-ups under a hill, where they would vanish, never to be seen again . . .

Inevitably, Franny would start humming with her fingers in her ears, and Will would shove his head under his pillow, and Poppy would begin arguing with her mother, saying that these horrifying tales could not actually be true, even as her heart beat a little faster.

"How could fairies dance by the moonlight without anyone seeing them?" she would demand. "How could people not notice that a ring of stones suddenly appeared in the landscape, then disappeared five days later?"

Finally Mrs. Malone had decided, with a sigh of

regret, not to use folktales as bedtime stories any-more. "They're too young to understand the deep truth hidden inside the old folklore," she said to Mr. Malone. "We just need to wait until they're a little more grown-up, that's all."

Poppy had overheard this conversation and had, even at six years old, scoffed at the idea that she would ever believe such silly stories.

But now, watching the dancers in the flicker-ing firelight, she could understand how people in the past—people who didn't know as much about science as she did—might have thought they were strange, otherworldly beings.

Poppy's attention focused on the youngest person in the group, the girl who seemed (from a distance, anyway) to be about her own age. She had a small face with a pointed chin and long red hair that hung almost to her waist in a mass of curls that glowed copper in the firelight. She seemed to be wearing a piece of fabric that wrapped around her body and was tied with a knot at the shoulder.

Poppy thought that it was a sarong, a piece of material that women in tropical parts of the world wrap around their body to fashion a dress. (She was surprised that she knew this. Poppy knew a great deal about many topics, but dresses was not one of them. She had, however, recently been the unwilling victim of a fashion makeover, conducted by Franny. Most of that horrible afternoon was just a blur now, but she had retained a few completely useless bits of information.)

The two older girls had secret smiles on their faces, as if they knew something no one else did and were quite smug about it, but the girl who was Poppy's age just looked annoyed. It was an expression that Poppy recognized. She was pretty sure she had worn it on her own face from time to time. It was the expression of someone who was being forced to take part in something she had no interest in (a paranormal investigation in Poppy's case, a weird dance in the woods for this girl).

"Don't stop dancing, Nerissa!" the silver-haired woman with the harp said encouragingly.

"Remember, the circle must not be broken, my dear. And you're doing wonderfully well, truly you are!"

Even from a distance, Poppy could see the girl Nerissa scowl.

"I hate this, Coralie," she said to the older woman. "I can't dance, I never *could* dance, I never will be *able* to dance—"

"Nonsense," the older woman said briskly. "You just need to try a little harder."

Nerissa sighed but raised her arms in an unenthusiastic manner and began shuffling around the fire again.

The two other dancers exchanged amused glances. They were around Franny's age. In fact, one looked a bit like Franny, with her curly blond hair and upturned nose.

The second girl had short, spiky black hair, a pointed chin, and a superior expression that made her look remarkably like a cat.

"Maybe you're trying a little too hard, Nerissa," the blond girl said sweetly. "You should focus on relaxing your shoulders. See? Like this." As she swayed gracefully around the fire, she turned her head to gaze in admiration at the movements of her arms, just as Franny would have done.

Nerissa rolled her eyes. "Thanks for the suggestion, Ariadne," she said. "But if I start thinking about waving my arms in the air, I'll trip over my own feet, you know I will."

The dark-haired girl snickered.

Nerissa turned to glare at her. "Stop laughing, Kali!" she snapped. "You're always making fun of me and I'm sick of it."

Kali's expression shifted to one that was so serious that, even from a distance, Poppy could tell she was mocking Nerissa. "I wasn't laughing at you," Kali protested in an injured voice. "I want to help you. Why don't you try moving your hips a little bit," she said. "Like this . . ."

Kali joined Ariadne and they began dancing around the fire again. They dipped and swayed and whirled like leaves blowing in a breeze. Watching them, Poppy felt as if she were falling under a spell.

Then Nerissa, frowning in concentration, tried

to copy their moves. It only took three stumbling steps, accompanied by a few hopelessly awkward waves of her arms, to break the spell.

Nerissa stopped and let her arms drop to her side. "I can't do that," she said to the woman named Coralie, nodding toward Ariadne and Kali, who were still circling the fire. "No matter how hard I try, I'll never be able to do that."

Coralie frowned. A cloud crossed in front of the moon, making the night even darker.

"You would not have a problem if you would just apply yourself," she said in exactly the same exasperated tone Mrs. Malone had used last fall when Will had gotten a D in math (he claimed that long division was so stupefying that he fell asleep every time he tried to do his homework). "You simply need to embrace your true nature. Do that, and all will fall into place."

But the girl Nerissa shook her head gloomily. "I've tried," she said. "Nothing works."

"Maybe that's because your great-great-grandmother fell in love with that sailor in Scotland, then ran off and married him," Ariadne said in a teasing voice. She glanced at Kali, and they shared an amused look.

"That's right," said Kali. "Maybe you've got a bit too much of his blood running through your veins—"

"I don't! Stop saying that!" snapped Nerissa. "Just because I'm not very good at dancing, that doesn't mean—"

"Of course it doesn't." Coralie's tone was soothing now, although she shot a warning look at the other two girls over Nerissa's head. "Kali, Ariadne, how many times have I told you— Nerissa is your little sister. You should help her and encourage her."

Ariadne's perfect little rosebud mouth pouted, and Kali raised one dark eyebrow rebelliously, but they both said in unison, "Sorry, Coralie. Sorry, Nerissa."

Coralie waited a moment, then nodded, her hair flashing silver in the firelight. "Well, then," she said. "We begin again—"

As the dancers wound their way in a circle once more, Poppy's gaze slid past the circle of firelight to the trees surrounding the clearing. There was one huge old oak tree, gnarled and twisted, that seemed to sparkle. Poppy looked closer. As the firelight danced and flickered in the dark, she saw that there were sequined cloaks draped on the branches. At that moment, a breeze sprung up and the cloaks swayed, flashing silver and blue and moving almost as if they were living things. . . .

This was so beautiful, and so unexpected, that Poppy gasped.

Instantly, she knew she had made a mistake.

Every one of the figures in the clearing turned their heads in her direction. For one frozen instant, she thought that, if she stayed very, very still, she might escape detection.

But then, somewhere behind her, she heard Will shout, "Poppy! Where are you?"

Without meaning to, she turned her head—and she was discovered.

She heard someone call out something. The

words were indistinct, but the note of alarm was clear enough.

All four figures ran to the oak tree and grabbed their cloaks, then raced toward the shore. They moved incredibly fast, like raindrops sliding down a window. With one fluid move, three of them dove into the water and were gone. Only the youngest hesitated on the shore, still holding her cloak in her arms.

Poppy blinked. The dark water of the lake was unnaturally still. There wasn't a ripple to show that the surface had just been disturbed.

Shivering, she picked up her paddle and started to turn her kayak around. Without even thinking about it, she found that she was paddling gently, as if not to disturb the water too much. As if not to let anything underneath the surface know where she was . . .

A hand shot up from the water and grabbed the side of her kayak. A second later, a head emerged. It was the silver-haired woman. She was floating in the water next to Poppy, her icy blue eyes fixed on Poppy's face, smiling strangely.

"Hello, my darling," she crooned. "What are you doing out here on the water, so far from home?"

"N-nothing," Poppy stuttered.

Another head emerged from the water, then another. They were the dancers from the clearing, only they were no longer smiling. They stared at her with distrust and dislike.

"Spying, more like it," said Kali, the girl with the dark spiky hair. "What shall we do with her?"

The coldness in her voice made Poppy gulp.

Kali reached over the side of the kayak and grabbed Poppy's arm with a hand that felt as cold as ice. Poppy squeaked and tried to pull away, but the girl's grip was strong.

"Pull her into the water," Kali said in a deliberate voice, as if she'd given the matter a great deal of thought. "Pull her under the waves."

"You can't do that!" Poppy cried out. "If you hurt me, you'll get in trouble."

Kali gave her a sly look. "Will we, now? And who is here to see what happens to you?"

Poppy pulled back with all her strength, which only made the kayak rock to one side and almost capsize.

Kali laughed. It was a laugh like none other Poppy had ever heard. It made her heart race with terror.

"It looks as if she might do our work for us, it does indeed," she said, her eyes gleaming with malice.

"Stop it!"

Startled, Poppy jerked her head up to see Nerissa, who was now standing on a large rock at the edge of the cove and staring at Poppy.

"Don't hurt her! She didn't do anything. Let her go."

Poppy felt a wave of gratitude wash over her. Finally, someone was saying something reasonable! Now if only the others would listen—

But Kali just laughed her bone-chilling laugh again. "Ah, Nerissa, you have such a warm heart," she said mockingly. "Full of compassion and pity and kindness!"

"No, I don't!" Nerissa snapped. "But if we hurt her, we'll only be bringing trouble upon ourselves, will we not? And how smart is that?"

The others broke into peals of laughter.

"Poor Nerissa, *mer* on the outside and mortal in the middle," called out Ariadne.

A clear, cold voice broke through the murmurs. "Nerissa is right," said the older woman. "Let the girl go."

Poppy thought she had never heard the word "girl" said with such disdain. Before she had a chance to feel insulted, however, the grip on her arm loosened.

She pulled away and rubbed the spot where Kali had been holding her. It felt cold to the touch, as if she'd been holding an ice pack there.

"Who are you, anyway?" she asked. Her voice wavered and she cleared her throat before adding, "What are you doing here?"

No one answered. They all stared at her. Poppy stared back into their blank eyes and felt a prickle on the back of her neck. She could hear her mother's voice saying, "Centuries ago, people used to say they had encountered the uncanny when they had, in fact, encountered the paranormal. The surefire way to know that you were in the presence of the uncanny, they said, was when the hairs on the back of your neck stood up. . . ."

"Poppy!" Will's voice called out.

Coralie's head turned sharply in the direction of his voice.

"Dive." The older woman's voice snapped out with an air of command.

There were three small splashes and they were gone.

Only Nerissa remained where she was, standing on the rock. She was looking at Poppy with intense curiosity.

"Poppy!" Henry yelled. "Where are you?"

Nerissa blinked and turned her head sharply in the direction of the voices. Then she flung the cloak around her shoulders in one graceful move, stood on her tiptoes, and dove off the rock into the lake.

The whole thing happened so quickly that Poppy almost missed it.

She stared at the spot where the girl had disappeared.

"Oh, there you are!" Henry's voice sounded both exasperated and relieved. "Why didn't you answer us? Didn't you hear us calling you?"

She turned to see Henry and Will paddling into the cove.

"Yeah, what's wrong with you?" Will said. "We've been looking for you forever! Mom and Dad are going nuts. They picked up some kind of weird blip in the sky, just south of here, and they want to raise anchor and head after it."

"They said the blip was zigzagging all over the sky!" said Henry excitedly. "I can't believe we might have found a UFO on our very first day on the lake!"

Will gave him a pitying look. "Don't get your hopes too high. The last time they thought they'd seen a UFO, it turned out to be the local TV station's traffic helicopter."

Henry was not willing to give up so easily. "But your dad said the flight plan was completely abnormal! Not like any plane or helicopter known to man!"

"Henry, Henry, Henry." Will shook his head sadly. "He always says that. Trust me, we're not going to encounter anything strange this week—"

"Did you see her?" Poppy interrupted. "Did you see that girl?"

Will and Henry exchanged puzzled looks.

"What girl?" Henry asked.

"The one who was standing right there." She pointed to the rock. "She just dove into the lake."

"Don't tell me *you're* seeing things now," said Will. "It's bad enough that Mom and Dad keep getting fooled—"

"I'm not imagining things!" Poppy's voice was tense. "You'll never believe what I just saw—"

"Yeah, yeah, we want to hear all about it," said Will. "Later. Mom and Dad sent us on a mission and the mission was to find you and get back to the houseboat."

"Listen—" Poppy began, but Will and Henry had already turned their kayak around and were paddling out of the cove.

With a quick thrust of her paddle, she followed them. But as she left the cove behind, she glanced back over her shoulder one last time.

She knew what she had seen.

When the girl put on her cloak, it had seemed to melt into her body, covering her shoulders and legs with scales that sparkled in the moonlight. And when she dove into the water, a large, spangled tail had flipped into the air before disappearing under the waves.

As hard as it was to believe, Poppy was absolutely certain of one thing: She had just seen her first mermaid.

Chapter
SIX

As soon as Poppy set foot on the deck of the houseboat, she knew that no one would have the time or patience to listen to anything she had to say.

Mrs. Malone, her eyes bright, was waving a printout of a photo in the air.

"Look at this image," she cried. "It's clear as day! There's a UFO in the skies above us!"

Poppy took the paper from her hand. She stared at it for a long moment, then raised one eyebrow and said, "It's a white smudge."

Her mother snatched it back. "That's what a blazing light that flashes across the sky looks like in a photograph," she said. "And look!" She stabbed a finger at the paper. "See these little dots here? If you connect them to the bright light, it forms a triangle."

She paused and gave them all a meaningful look.

"A *triangle*," she repeated, in case they had missed her point.

"But you can play connect-the-dots with any random number of points and come up with a shape," Poppy said reasonably. "Triangle, square, trapezoid, polygon, rhomboid—"

"I think you've made your point, Poppy, thank you," said Mr. Malone, who had emerged from the galley in time to hear this. "However, you're ignoring a key factor. Forty-three percent of UFO witnesses report that what they saw was triangular in shape."

He stopped long enough to give her a gloating look, then added, "Makes you think, doesn't it?"

"Yes," Poppy snapped. "It makes me think that people are seeing what they want to see."

"That can't be right," said Mr. Malone. "Why,

you ask?" (Poppy didn't bother pointing out that she hadn't.) He leaned forward and said triumphantly, "Because most people don't want to see aliens. They're too afraid!"

"That's true," said Mrs. Malone. "Which is ridiculous, really, when you think of how much we could learn from any creatures who have the technology to zip over to Earth from who knows how many light-years away!"

Poppy took a deep breath. "Have you ever thought you might be looking in the wrong place?" she asked carefully.

"What do you mean?"

"I mean . . . well, what if the strange creatures aren't zipping around over our heads in little spacecraft? What if they're a little closer to home? Maybe even"—she pointed at the lake—"down there?"

"You didn't buy all that guff that Oliver was dishing out about lake monsters, did you?" scoffed Mr. Malone.

Poppy blushed. "I don't believe anything anybody says without seeing the evidence," she said stiffly. "Especially not anything that Professor Asquith says. He's only interested in TV ratings."

"Ha! Quite right, too!" said Mr. Malone. "You see, Lucille, even a young girl like Poppy can see through Oliver's never-ending quest for fame."

"Now, dear," said Mrs. Malone, sounding a trifle annoyed. "There's no need to be rude about poor Oliver. I admit, he can be quite imaginative, but he has had his successes."

"Only because the viewing public has no taste." Mr. Malone's mood had swung, as it usually did when Oliver Asquith was praised, from delight to utter gloom. "No taste and absolutely no under-standing of the field of paranormal investigation. I blame our education system. What are kids taught in school these days? To answer multiple-choice questions and march in lockstep down the halls of academe! There's absolutely no attention being paid to clear thinking. Why, I remember when I was young—"

Poppy tried to get the conversation back on track before Mr. Malone started talking about the rigors of first grade, and how he'd mastered multiplication and long division by his eighth birthday.

"Anyway, I wasn't talking about a lake monster," she interrupted. "There are other aquatic creatures, you know. I mean, what if you thought you saw, say—"

"Did someone see the monster?" Rolly was half asleep, but he got up from the deck chair and staggered toward them, his fishing pole clutched tightly in his hands. "Where is it?"

"*Shh, shh,* go back to sleep," said Mrs. Malone soothingly. "There's nothing to see, nothing going on at all."

Rolly stopped in his tracks and watched as Mr. Malone started the engine.

"Where are we going?" he asked.

"To another part of the lake," said Mrs. Malone. "Now why don't you lie down and think some happy thoughts, and before you know it you'll be in dreamland!"

Poppy shook her head, but said nothing. Her mother had been suggesting this ever since Rolly was one month old. It had never worked, for two reasons. One was that Rolly had decided, apparently on the day he was born, that he couldn't waste any time sleeping because he had too much to do in his life.

The second reason Mrs. Malone's strategy was useless, of course, was that Rolly didn't think happy thoughts. Cunning thoughts, yes. Obsessive thoughts, certainly. Stubborn thoughts, without a doubt. But happy thoughts? No.

"I don't want to nod off," he said. "I don't want to go to dreamland. I don't want to sleep at all, not ever!"

"You have made that abundantly clear over the years," said Mr. Malone through gritted teeth. "I don't suppose you'd try counting sheep?"

Rolly gave him a black look. "I don't like sheep."

"Well, try counting lake monsters, then," Mr. Malone snapped.

"Now *there's* a brainstorm!" Mrs. Malone said brightly. "In fact, why don't you just close your eyes for a few minutes. You don't have to actually sleep. You just need to rest for a few minutes and the best way to do that is with your eyes closed."

Rolly thought this over, as if testing the idea for a trap, but finally nodded. "Okay," he said. "I'll rest. As long as I don't have to sleep." He fell back on the deck chair, screwed his eyes closed, and crossed his arms belligerently, as if daring sleep to overtake him.

For several minutes, everyone worked in silence, scarcely daring to breathe. And then, the most delightful sound interrupted the quiet of the night. It was a deep buzzing that sounded like a hive of irritated bees. It was the sound of Rolly snoring.

"Finally!" Mr. Malone said.

"*Shh.*" Mrs. Malone held up a warning hand. "Quietly, quietly! We don't want him to wake up. . . ."

Everyone tiptoed to the far side of the boat, where Mrs. Malone returned to the matter of the photos.

"It can't be just a coincidence," she insisted. "Ten of the last fifteen sightings in this area have involved three sets of moving lights, all shaped like triangles—"

"Maybe they were plane lights," said Poppy, adding helpfully, "You know, those lights on the wings and the tail? The ones that keep planes from running into one another? Have you ever noticed how they look like a triangle?"

Mrs. Malone ignored this. "Witnesses said that the lights moved at a tremendous rate of speed. Faster than any plane they'd ever seen. One minute the lights were over there"—she waved toward the eastern shore—"and the next minute—*whoosh!*— they had shot across to the other side of the lake and then disappeared!"

"I think I heard a story like that once," said Henry, interested. "But it happened a long time ago. One of my friends at school said his grandfather saw the lights when he was a kid."

"Oh, the sightings have been going on for years," said Mrs. Malone. She pushed her glasses up her nose, her eyes sparkling with excitement. "I've been doing some research online. There are stories about UFO sightings in the local newspapers dating back to the eighteen hundreds. In fact, five of the top twenty cities around the world that have reported UFOs are right here in Texas! And Austin is number six on the list! Some people say—"

"Uh-huh," said Will. "So, are we going to get something to eat? Because Henry and I are starving."

"There's fruit in the fridge," Mrs. Malone said. "Oh, and some granola bars! That will help boost our energy and keep us going! All night, if need be!"

"Fruit! Granola bars!" Will said in disgust. "I thought Dad was going to make spaghetti."

"With meatballs," added Poppy, who had been looking forward to them all day.

"Change in plans," said Mr. Malone briskly. "We'll have it tomorrow. But tonight—we are on the hunt!"

Poppy and Will exchanged exasperated looks. They knew from bitter experience that it was not a good sign when one of their parents said, "We are on the hunt!" It meant they were caught up in an enthusiasm so overwhelming that it overpowered the need for food, sleep, or bathing. Poppy still remembered the weeklong Bigfoot stakeout on a West Texas ranch. Every night, each Malone had been dowsed with skunk oil meant to mask their human smell, directed to a tree, and told to climb to the highest branch possible. It had taken weeks for the stink to wear off and, in the end, all they saw were several herds of deer and a disgruntled javelina pig.

Mr. Malone grabbed a navigational map from the table. "We are paranormal investigators!" he finished, snapping it open with a flourish. "When we see a mysterious light in the sky, we don't lollygag about!"

"No, sir!" said Henry.

Will glared at him and shook his head. But Henry didn't know the secret signs and signals that Will and Poppy had developed to silently communicate with each other. He didn't know that Will was trying to say, "Be quiet! Don't encourage them!" And even if he *had* known . . .

Poppy was watching Henry closely. His eyes were sparkling, his cheeks were flushed, and he was bouncing on his toes. With a sinking heart, she spotted the telltale signs of a newly hatched paranormal fanatic.

She sidled up to him. "Don't get too excited," she warned him. "Most UFO sightings are weather balloons, you know. Or military aircraft. Or the planet Venus."

Henry shrugged this off. "*Most* of them are," he agreed. "But what if this one isn't? What if it's the real thing?"

Poppy rolled her eyes.

"Oh no," Will groaned. "You've gone to the dark side."

"That's the spirit!" said Mr. Malone, clapping Henry on the back. "Come on, why don't you help me chart our course. Now, the light was seen heading south by southwest—"

He pointed helpfully into the darkness. "Mrs. Malone followed it across the sky with our AlienScope."

"What's that?"

Mr. Malone nodded toward Poppy. "Ask our scientist," he said genially. "She invented it."

Henry turned to Poppy. "You did?" he asked in surprise. "But if you don't believe in aliens—"

"I don't!" said Poppy, annoyed. "But I like inventing stuff. And anyway"—she shrugged, embarrassed—"it was Mother's Day."

Mrs. Malone smiled fondly at Poppy. "So sweet," she said.

Henry picked up the AlienScope to take a closer look. "It looks pretty cool," he said, turning it over in his hands. "How did you make it?"

Poppy tried to look modest, but a small, pleased smiled lifted one corner of her mouth. "I just took a radar detector gun and added a few hacks," she said. "My theory is that, if UFOs really existed, they might emit some kind of electromagnetic waves. That could explain why witnesses often report that their car engines stalled when they saw a UFO, for example. The tricky part was figuring out how to tell the difference between natural electromagnetic forces and those that might have been created by an alien spacecraft. It was an interesting problem and I was stuck a couple of times, but then one day I happened to find a book at the library and—"

"The AlienScope was created," Will said briskly. "Patent pending. When are we going to *eat*?"

"Grab an apple," suggested Mrs. Malone as she pointed her AlienScope at the sky. "That will tide you over. Emerson, do you want me to weigh anchor?"

"Yes, we've got it now," said Mr. Malone. "I'm setting a course for ten degrees south by thirty degrees southwest. Full speed ahead!"

Chapter
SEVEN

"Of course, when I said 'full speed ahead,' I didn't mean 'full speed into the closest sandbar and please try to hit a tree while you're at it,'" said Mr. Malone. He gave a little chuckle. "I'm afraid my family takes everything I say a bit too literally."

"Uh-huh." Officer Dan Deetline of the Austin Police Department jotted down a few notes.

The other Malones were standing by the railing, leaning over the water to inspect the bow of the houseboat. It had been crunched by a startling collision with a sandbank. An old oak tree, hard as iron, had stood on the bank, half submerged in water. Now it seemed to be clutching the front of the houseboat in its branches.

The officer glanced up from his notebook and gave Mr. Malone a stern look. "What I don't get is why you were saying 'full speed ahead' in the first place. It was too dark to see anything, and these houseboats aren't exactly made for racing. What was so all-fired important you had to get over to this side of the lake so quick?"

"Well, you see, my son Will was at the helm," Mr. Malone began, then he chuckled again.

Poppy recognized this chuckle. It was the one her father always used when confronted by Authority.

This happened rather often in the course of a paranormal investigation. A highway patrolman wanted to know why he was driving ninety miles an hour on West Virginia mountain roads (he was pursuing Moth Man). A security guard wanted to know why he was trying to enter an office building after midnight (he hoped to capture the ghostly whispers of an accountant who loved his job so much he kept working—forty years after he'd died). And a police officer wanted to know why he was trespassing on a farmer's land (he was so focused on his pursuit of a zombie that was rumored to be roaming about the woods that he hadn't even seen the "Keep Out!" signs).

The chuckle was supposed to sound amused, carefree, lighthearted. It was the chuckle of a man who couldn't imagine why he was being questioned by Authority.

Poppy had never seen The Chuckle work. She searched Officer Deetline's face to see if her father might do better with it tonight.

But Officer Deetline's expression was stony.

"Uh-huh," he said. "So you're saying this is your son's fault?"

"Er, well," Mr. Malone began, flustered.

"Oh, sure, it was all my fault," Will said hotly. "This whole shipwreck was my mistake. Just like it was my mistake when you pointed at that light in the sky and yelled that the aliens would get away if I didn't open up the throttle—"

Officer Deetline's expression didn't change, but Poppy thought that she saw one eyebrow move up ever so slightly. "Aliens?"

"Yes, we were chasing a UFO," Mr. Malone said. He turned to Will and added testily, "And I remember quite well what I said. Naturally, I assumed that you were capable of using good old-fashioned common sense."

"And I'm sure I was in the wrong when I followed your orders to make a sharp turn to starboard so that Mom could get a better angle with the AlienScope," Will finished heatedly. "It's all clear to me now. We wouldn't be about to sink to the bottom of the lake and die horrible drowning deaths if it weren't for me and the way I actually listen to what you say and then do it!"

"Now, now," said Mrs. Malone in what was clearly meant to be a soothing voice. "I just checked out the cabin. There is a tiny, tiny leak, but the water's not coming in terribly fast. I doubt we'll sink, will we, Officer?"

Officer Deetline's eyebrows lowered (Poppy assumed that he did this to relax a bit; they certainly couldn't go any higher). "Probably not. You weren't moving that fast. But you're going to have to be towed to the dock. And before that happens, I'll need to take some photos for the police report. . . ."

The officer stepped off the houseboat deck and onto his police launch, then maneuvered closer to the area of the houseboat that had sustained the most damage. As soon as he was out of earshot, Mr. Malone glowered at Poppy and said, "I told you not to call them. Now we're going to lose at least a day of our investigation."

"You have to report an accident immediately. It's the law," countered Poppy. "Plus, we need a police report so that the insurance company will pay for the repairs. Plus, we couldn't get off the sandbar by ourselves. Plus—"

"All right, Poppy, I think we've got the point," said Mr. Malone.

"I don't imagine it will take long to do such a minor repair," Mrs. Malone said soothingly. "I'm sure we'll be back on the hunt before you know it. . . ."

"I can't believe it!" Mr. Malone stood on the dock, his hands on his hips, and stared at the houseboat in disgust. "Three whole days lost! And for what? A tiny crack!"

The boat mechanic, who had just finished the list of everything he had to fix, shook his head gloomily.

"You got a hole in your hull," he said. "That's not a good thing for a boat to have."

"It's a crack, not a hole, and you can barely see it!" protested Mr. Malone. "It's not as if the boat flooded, you know. It just got a bit damp."

"Now, dear," Mrs. Malone said. "Safety comes first. And this will give us time to analyze our initial findings. We've already got at least ten hours of film to sort through. If you look at it the right way, being in dry dock for a while is really a blessing in disguise!"

Poppy, Will, and Franny exchanged looks of alarm. They did not consider this a blessing of any sort, disguised or otherwise. They knew very well that ten hours of video could take three days to analyze. Mr. Malone always insisted on stopping the tape every few seconds to stare at the screen, looking for anomalies. And Mrs. Malone had a theory that watching tape in reverse revealed hidden clues, which meant that not only did she rewind constantly, but she did so in slow motion.

"Ashley asked me to stay on their boat for a few nights," Franny said quickly. "It turns out that a lot of her friends have seen strange lights out at the lake, too. She's been texting them all afternoon. I thought I could take a laptop with me and tape their stories for our files. . . ."

"That's a brilliant idea!" Mrs. Malone said, beaming. "You see, Emerson? This little setback will actually give us an opportunity to do background research that we would have had to do anyway."

"Turncoat!" Will hissed. "Traitor!"

Franny tossed her blond curls and cast a superior smile at Will. "You're not the only one who can think fast," she said sweetly.

"Henry and I could hike along the shore," Will said quickly. "You know, look for signs that spaceships have landed. Scorched earth, mysterious crop circles in the underbrush, that sort of thing."

"That's a good idea," said Poppy. "I could bring the Geiger counter and take readings—"

"Isn't it wonderful how the children are willing to pitch in and help, Emerson?" said Mrs. Malone.

"I notice no one is volunteering to sit at home and analyze film," grumbled Mr. Malone.

"There's a trailhead right over there by that road," Henry said to Will, pointing. "We could start there and hike all the way to the boat club. I did that last year with my dad."

"Excellent," said Will. "Let me get my compass." He began searching through his duffel bag.

"I can get the Geiger counter from the boat—" Poppy began.

"Nah, that's okay," said Will. "If we keep stopping to take readings, we'll just slow down our investigation."

Henry was bouncing on his toes as if he couldn't wait to hit the trail. "Maybe next time," he said. "I'll call my aunt and ask her to pick us up when we're done, okay?"

And with that, Will and Henry ran off.

"You're going to wish you had a Geiger counter," Poppy muttered darkly as she watched them go. "When you find a circle of smoking, scorched earth, you're going to wish you had a way to measure ionizing radiation over time—"

Then she felt a hand on her shoulder. She turned to see Mrs. Malone smiling at her.

"We really need someone to research all the UFO sightings reported in this area," she said. "After all, if this is an alien hot spot, last night wasn't the first time they visited. I know how you love to go to the library, so I was wondering . . ."

Poppy sighed. "Sure," she said. "That sounds like fun, too."

Chapter
EIGHT

The next morning all the Malones got up, got dressed, and got away from the house as soon as they could. Mr. Malone sped off to the dock, where he planned to personally oversee the houseboat repair, urging the workers on so that they would complete it ahead of schedule. Franny went back to the lake to spend the day with Ashley. Even Will managed to be out of bed by eight o'clock, ready to head over to Henry's house, where Henry's aunt was going to drive them back to the lake to resume their hike.

"Be sure to get home in time for dinner," Mrs. Malone said as Will dashed through the kitchen. She pulled a frozen chicken from the freezer and thumped it on the kitchen table. "We're having coq au vin with roasted vegetables—"

"Thanks for the warning," said Will. "I'll put the fire department on speed dial."

"I don't think that's quite fair," said Mrs. Malone. "The recipe your grandmother sent me said that igniting brandy adds extra flavor. How was I to know that your father added an extra cup when I wasn't looking?"

"Hey, I happen to like the sound of sirens during dinner," said Will, grabbing the piece of toast that had just popped up from the toaster. "It adds atmosphere."

"Will!" said Poppy, who had been making the toast for herself. "That was my breakfast."

"Thanks. Remind me to pay you back some day." Will grinned and ran out of the house, letting the screen door slam shut behind him.

Mrs. Malone sat down and opened the little memo book that she used to write her To Do lists each day. "Well, at least I'll have a few minutes of peace and quiet to do some planning," she said to Poppy.

"Things have been in such a whirl that I haven't had a moment to think about the Machu Picchu trip your father and I are planning or go to the grocery store or start on new research or anything!"

She picked up a pencil stub, gazed into space for a moment, then began jotting down notes. Poppy grumpily threw another piece of bread in the toaster and stood frowning at it, her arms crossed.

For a few minutes, there was no sound in the kitchen except an occasional thump from upstairs, where Rolly was supposed to be getting dressed. (Both Poppy and Mrs. Malone ignored the thumps; it was only the sound of crashes or breaking glass that caused real concern.)

Eventually, Mrs. Malone looked over at Poppy and said, "You know, the toast won't get done any sooner because you're staring at it."

"I'm not staring at the toast; I'm *thinking*," Poppy said, keeping her eyes fixed on the toaster.

"I know, dear, you always are," said Mrs. Malone. "But if you're thinking about Henry—"

"I'm not!"

"Of course not," Mrs. Malone agreed. "I'm just saying that if you *were*, I'd imagine you'd be thinking about how nice a friend he is and how you can do things with him on your own sometimes, just as Will can do things with him on his own."

Poppy's eyes slid sideways to look at her mother. "I might be thinking that," she said, "if I bothered to think about him at all. Which I don't."

"Naturally you don't," Mrs. Malone said. "It would be a wonder if you did! You have so many other, more important things to think about—"

"I do!" said Poppy. "Millions of more important things!"

"You know what always gets my mind off my troubles?" asked Mrs. Malone in a cheery voice.

Poppy gave her a suspicious glance. "I don't have troubles."

"Analyzing hours and hours of videotape," said Mrs. Malone, beaming. "Before you know it, your mind has gone completely blank! I always find that a delightful sensation."

"I already have research plans, remember?" said

Poppy, snatching the toast from the toaster and burning her fingers in the process. "Ow. I'm going to do a historical survey of UFO sightings at the library."

"Oh yes, of course." Mrs. Malone nodded. She looked at the list she had been writing and sighed. "Still, if you did want to stay home, I'd be glad of the help. I don't know where I'll find the time to do all this, I really don't—"

She was interrupted by Rolly, who appeared at the kitchen door clutching a bow and arrow. The arrow had a stone arrowhead on one end and bright feathers on the other. He was also, Poppy noted, wearing a pink spangled tutu which she thought she recognized from a dance recital she had been forced to appear in when she was six.

Mrs. Malone's eyes widened. She dropped her notebook on the table and said in a strangled voice, "Rolly, put down that arrow at once!"

"Why?" His beady eyes got even beadier as he tried to stare Mrs. Malone down.

"Because that is your father's," said Mrs. Malone, who began edging toward him. "He brought it back from his trip to Massachusetts, when he researched that roving band of Pukwudgies. . . ."

"So?" said Rolly. "He's not using it now."

Poppy didn't bother to listen to the argument that was brewing. Instead, she spread some peanut butter on her toast and sat down at the table to eat. She picked up her mother's notebook and flipped it open, just in case there was anything interesting on today's To Do list.

The first item was dull: grocery shopping.

Milk (remember pint of cream for fairy dishes)
Eggs
Bigfoot bait—1 lb. chicken livers, 1/2 lb. rabbit
      kidneys, 2–3 ham hocks
Peanut butter—<u>large</u> jar
Sun god offering for Machu Picchu—maize (or
      just can of creamed corn?)
BREAD!!!

As Poppy read, Mrs. Malone gingerly squeezed behind her chair and headed toward Rolly, saying,

"But that bow is very valuable. It's not a toy for little boys to play with."

"I'm not little," Rolly growled. "And I'm not playing. I'm going to use it to get Mugwump." He looked thoughtful. "Is it hard to shoot a fish?"

"Yes, indeed. In fact, it's quite difficult," said Mrs. Malone, moving a little closer. "Practically impossible!"

Poppy rolled her eyes. If there was one way to make sure Rolly would do something, it was to tell him that it was impossible. She turned her attention back to her mother's list. As usual, Mrs. Malone's mind only focused on household chores for a short time before wandering to the more interesting aspects of paranormal research:

Get proton precession magnetometer fixed

(And it was about time, Poppy thought. The proton precession magnetometer had been wonky for months, ever since Mr. Malone had decided to use it to find ancient burial grounds that might, with luck, have a curse attached to them. Unfortunately, he had been so immersed in his search that he had tripped over a rock, causing both him and the magnetometer to crash to the ground. This, he later said, was positive proof that his curse theory was true.)

Poppy scanned the next few items on her mother's list.

E-mail U. of Edinburgh research library—any
     new tapes of banshee wails?
Phone Eileen re: zombie invasion (send crate of
     blowtorches? Get-well card?)

She shook her head and made a tutting sound under her breath. Mrs. Malone lived in hopes of finding someone, somewhere, who had managed to capture a banshee wail on tape. It was a frivolous hope, of course. People who said they had heard a banshee's eerie wailing—well, they simply had too much imagination. Just like Mrs. Malone's college friend Eileen, who had called last week in hysterics.

Zombies! Poppy thought with disgust. Eileen had probably heard nothing more sinister than a bunch of cows. Their mooing could sound like the hollow groans of the undead, if a person were inclined to believe in that. . . .

"Rolly, dear, *please* give the bow and arrow to me," said Mrs. Malone, a desperate edge entering her voice. "Pukwudgies put poison on their arrowheads. It's quite deadly."

But Rolly wasn't listening. His eyes narrowed as he notched the arrow in the bow.

"Rolly, did you hear me?" Mrs. Malone said sharply. "Deadly! Poison!"

Rolly stared at the frozen chicken and pulled back the bowstring.

Ah! Poppy brightened as she read the last item on the list.

Covered dish supper—pineapple surprise

Mrs. Malone's desserts were always a hit at school fund-raisers, church suppers, and psychic society potlucks—and she always made an extra batch for the Malones to enjoy at home.

"Hey, are we having pineapple surprise tonight?" Poppy asked.

"Assuming we are all still alive, yes," snapped Mrs. Malone. "Rolly. . . ."

"Cool." Poppy swallowed her last bite of toast, grabbed her backpack, and headed out the door. "I'll ride my bike to the library," she called back over her shoulder. "See you later."

As she ran down the steps, she could hear Mrs. Malone saying, "Rolly, I'm warning you! If you shoot that chicken, we'll have liver for dinner— and you are going to eat *every single bite*. . . ."

An hour later, Poppy was slumped in a wooden cubicle at the library in front of a microfiche machine. She was staring at the images of old newspaper pages as she slowly turned the handle.

Usually she could get lost in doing research, but not today. Every five minutes, she'd realize that she had flipped past dozens of pages without seeing them. Then she would have to flip back to the last article she had read and force herself to concentrate.

She had read about airships that hovered over a small town thirty miles from Austin back in the 1890s, and strange lights that streaked across the sky in the 1950s, and reports of tiny figures with large heads that were spotted at night in the beam of a car's headlight, then vanished without a trace. She had read about one night in the 1980s when dozens of people claimed to see a huge object—two or three football fields long and triangular in shape, covered with blinking lights—glide slowly from the eastern horizon to the west.

After Poppy had found all the stories, printed them, and put them in her folder, she walked over to where books on folklore, legends, and myths were shelved. As she pulled down one book after another, flipping through the pages, she thought about what her father always said.

"When you begin any investigation, start with local legends," Mr. Malone would say. "There's generally a grain of truth in them. Someone saw something mysterious, maybe a few centuries earlier. They told their friends and family. Their children told their grandchildren. After a while, the story grew. Embroidery was added. It became too fantastic to be believed. But if you could go back to the original story—the one that was told right after the fact, when the person's heart was still pounding and his hair was still standing on end—well, maybe that story would sound real. Real enough to be believed. You just have to scrape off all the ornamentation and find the truth."

It sounded good in theory. But now that a day had passed, Poppy was starting to question herself.

Had she really seen mermaids?

Or was she just imagining things?

She took down a fat book with a faded green cover. The title on the spine had been gold, but most of the letters had been rubbed away. The spine was broken, and the cover was stained. Most people would have put the book back without even opening it. But Poppy was experienced in the ways of libraries and bookstores. She knew that the small, unnoticed, shabby little volume was often the one that had the most interesting information.

She turned to the title page. It read: *Mermaids in Myth, Legend, and Life.*

Poppy nodded to herself. This was exactly what she needed.

"Who knows how many people have heard the siren call of a mermaid? Most of those who have were never seen again. The lucky few who survived their mermaid encounter have said that they never saw a woman more lovely or heard a voice more sweet. Furthermore, they say the mermaid's song bewitches any man who hears it, so that he loses his senses and often leaps into the deepest ocean in order to follow it."

Poppy rolled her eyes and turned the page.

"There have been other stories as well," she read, "stories of mermaids that were seen walking on land. Some say mermaids can only leave the sea during an eclipse of the sun or a blue moon;

others have suggested that the mermaids were washed ashore during a storm and could not find their way home. At any rate, several men claimed to have married these mermaids and had children with them, although no one knows whether the children ended up choosing the land or the sea once they grew up. . . ."

Poppy wrinkled her nose and flipped to the section labeled "Hoaxes."

"Many mermaid sightings have been revealed as hoaxes," she read. "One of the most famous, of course, was the Feejee Mermaid displayed by P.T. Barnum, the famous American showman, businessman, and con artist. The mermaid was nothing more than the bodies of a large fish and a monkey which had been sewn together and mummified. Still, it managed to fool a good number of people who flocked to Barnum's circus to see it. . . ."

Poppy dropped the book to the table, shaking her head. "A Feejee Mermaid," she muttered to herself. "Honestly."

"It's ridiculous, isn't it?" a voice said over her shoulder.

Startled, Poppy turned around to see a girl standing behind her. She looked about Poppy's age. She had red hair pulled back in a long ponytail and bright green eyes. She wore a faded T-shirt, wrinkled shorts, and old tennis shoes with holes in the toes, and she had a battered canvas backpack slung over one shoulder. The only thing that didn't look old and ragged was a necklace made of tiny shells strung on a piece of twine. She stood with her head tilted to one side, smirking at the illustration of the Feejee Mermaid in Poppy's book.

"Totally ridiculous," said Poppy, pushing her chair back so that she could see the girl more clearly. "Are you interested in mermaids?"

The girl gave Poppy an odd, sidelong grin.

"You could say that," she said. "But even so, I'd never pay good money to see a creature that looked as daft as that."

Poppy glanced down at the book. "Yeah," she agreed. "Of course, this was back in the olden days, before nature shows on TV and science magazines and the Internet. People didn't know any better."

"Idjits," the girl declared with an annoyed shake of her head. "Just take a look at this!" She dropped her backpack to the floor, picked up another book from the desk, and gave a little sniff of disdain as she examined the cover. It showed an angelic-looking mermaid perched on a rock and simpering at a sailor on a ship.

"Totally daft," she said. "Who'd be sitting on a burning hot rock in the sun when they could be swimming? Who'd want to make cow eyes at a man?"

She held up the book so Poppy could see it, too.

"Especially a man who wears one of those little round sailor hats," she added.

But Poppy only half heard her. She was staring at the girl's hand.

There were delicate webs of skin stretched between each finger. A dark green bracelet of lake weed was wound around each wrist. In the dim light of the library, the girl's skin seemed to have a greenish blue tone.

"You—you . . ." Poppy's voice came out in a squeak. She cleared her throat and tried again. "You're the girl at the lake. I saw you dancing on the shore." She paused again, then said in a rush, "I saw you dive into the water."

The girl's grin widened. She raised one eyebrow. "Did you now?" she said. "That must have caught your attention. Someone deciding to take a swim when they were at a lake—"

"I know you're a mermaid," said Poppy, more loudly than she meant to.

"Shh," someone sitting at a table two bookshelves over hissed.

Now that Poppy realized who the girl was, she was surprised she hadn't recognized her right away. She'd had the same stormy expression on her face when the others had teased her about her dancing. . . .

Poppy snapped her fingers. "Nerissa," she said. "That's your name. Nerissa. What are you doing here?"

Nerissa's chin lifted defiantly. "I ran away."

"You did? Why?" Poppy frowned down at Nerissa's feet. "And I don't mean to be rude, but . . . how? What happened to your tail?"

Nerissa tossed her head. "All mermaids can walk on land when the conditions are right," she said. "You didn't learn about that in all your books, did you?"

"Well, actually—" Poppy began.

"It takes a blue moon," said Nerissa, "and a spirit of adventure, of course."

Poppy's fingers itched to pick up her pencil and start making notes, but she worried that it might offend Nerissa, so she just said, "But then why haven't more people met mermaids? There's a blue moon almost every year."

"I know!" said Nerissa. "You'd think they'd take advantage of it. But most mermaids are happy just hanging around in the same water for centuries, swimming with dolphins and teasing seals and sitting around on rocks combing their hair. And, of course, most mermaids think human beings are silly and kind of, well, dim. They're always joking about how easy it is to play tricks on people. So most of them aren't very interested in pretending to be one, even for a few days."

"Oh." Poppy tried not to sound as offended as she felt. "So if you think people are such idiots, why are you here?"

Nerissa's eyes widened in dismay. "I didn't mean to hurt your feelings," she said quickly. "I'm not like all the other mermaids. In fact, I've always wondered . . ." Her voice trailed off.

"Wondered what?" Poppy asked.

"I always wondered what it would be like to be mortal," Nerissa said in a low voice, her eyes shifting around the room as if she were afraid of being heard. "That's one of the reasons the others make fun of me."

Poppy thought back to that horrible moment when she thought the mermaids were going to pull her under the water. Nerissa had argued with them, told them they shouldn't do it. . . .

"They said you had a warm heart," she said. "That you were *mer* on the outside and—"

"Mortal in the middle," Nerissa finished bitterly. "Just because I think people are interesting and want to learn more about them. What's so wrong with being interested in the world and having a sense of curiosity and wanting to learn something once in a while, instead of just floating around in a lake somewhere?"

"Nothing," said Poppy.

"Honestly!" Nerissa was getting more worked up. "It drives me crazy, the way they don't care about anything except singing to the fish and looking at their reflections!"

She kicked the base of the bookshelf. Her mouth dropped open in surprise and began hopping on the other foot. "Ow. That *hurt*."

She sounded so astonished that Poppy laughed.

"Yeah, that's what happens when you get mad and kick something," she said. "You bruise your toes."

Nerissa frowned. The room darkened. Poppy glanced at the window and saw that the sky had clouded over.

"I should know," Poppy added hastily. "I've

done it a few times myself. I always think that kicking something will make me feel better, but it never does."

Nerissa relaxed and smiled slightly. A shaft of sunlight came through the window.

"I guess I'm not used to having feet," she admitted. "Or toes."

Nerissa wiggled her toes thoughtfully, then picked up *Mermaids in Myth, Legend, and Life*. "I'd like to read a book like this about mortals," she said. "Is there one in the library?"

"I don't think so," said Poppy. "I mean, there aren't really myths or legends about people."

Nerissa raised one eyebrow. "Oh no?" she said. "You mean you haven't heard the story about the boy who planted a bean and then climbed the beanstalk to the sky, where he met a giant?"

"That's just a fairy tale," said Poppy. "It's not true. It's not about a real person. And people aren't that interesting anyway."

"Not to you, because you are one," Nerissa

replied. "That's why you have no idea how strange you all are."

Poppy frowned. "I wouldn't say we're strange—" she began.

"Or how funny you sound," Nerissa added.

Poppy's frown deepened. "What do you mean by that?"

"Or how peculiar you look," added Nerissa.

"Hey, listen—" Poppy began hotly, but Nerissa didn't let her finish.

"Oh, there now. I've gone and insulted you without meaning to," she said quickly. "I'm sorry. Really, I'm fascinated by mortals."

"Right," Poppy said, frowning. "Even though we're all weird. And funny-sounding."

"Only because I don't know much about you," said Nerissa. She gave Poppy a meaningful look. "Just like you don't know much about mermaids. I bet you think we're a little odd, too."

Poppy felt her hurt feelings start to fade. "That's true," she admitted.

Nerissa leaned in closer. "I have an idea," she

said. "Let's make a deal. I'll tell you about mermaids, if you'll tell me about mortals."

Poppy thought about that for a moment. "So," she finally said, "where are you going to stay while you're here?"

"Stay?" asked Nerissa, puzzled.

"Yes. You can't just hang out on your own," Poppy explained. "People notice kids who don't seem to have anyplace to go. Sometimes they call the police."

For the first time, Nerissa looked unsure of herself, but she shrugged. "I'll hide," she said. "I'll make sure no one sees me."

"You could," agreed Poppy. She paused, then added, "Or you could come home with me."

Chapter
NINE

When Poppy and Nerissa walked up the sidewalk, the front door of the Malones' house was ajar and all the windows were open.

Poppy sighed. "The air-conditioning must be out again," she said to Nerissa. "Sorry. It's going to be pretty hot."

"I don't mind," Nerissa said brightly. Her mood seemed to change like the weather on a spring day. Her face was shining as she looked at the house. She ran lightly up the porch steps, dropped her backpack, and did a little pirouette. "I've never seen a mortal's home before. What's this?"

She pressed the doorbell. Her eyes widened

with delight when she heard the chime, and she pressed it again.

"Please," said Poppy. "Stop." (Mr. Malone had bought the doorbell from a specialty catalog; it rang the theme from the movie *Close Encounters of the Third Kind*. Poppy could never hear it without wincing and planned to quietly disable it at some point before she invited any new friends over.)

"It sounds so pretty," Nerissa was saying, just as Mrs. Malone came to the door.

"Oh, there you are, Poppy," she said, smiling over the top of her glasses. "And just in time, too!"

"In time for what?" asked Poppy warily.

But Mrs. Malone's gaze had moved to Nerissa. "Who is your new friend, dear?"

"This is Nerissa," said Poppy. "Nerissa, um"— she thought quickly—"De La Mer."

Two schools ago, she had taken French and learned that *de la mer* meant "of the sea." Poppy crossed her fingers and hoped that Nerissa would go along with the new last name she'd just been given.

She needn't have worried. Nerissa was opening and closing the metal flap of the mailbox next to the door, a look of utter fascination on her face.

"It's so nice to meet you, Nerissa," said Mrs. Malone. "What a lovely name. Would you like to join us?"

"For what?" Poppy asked, grabbing Nerissa's arm and pulling her away from the mailbox.

"We were just about to have a family brainstorm!" said Mrs. Malone, opening the screen door. "They're such fun, Nerissa. We'd love to have you help out. I'm sure you'll have wonderful ideas."

Poppy rolled her eyes, but Nerissa said, "Thank you, I'd be glad to help!" and practically skipped through the doorway in her delight.

Before Poppy could follow her, Mrs. Malone whispered, "I'm so glad you've made a new friend, Poppy. Where does she live?"

"Oh, a few blocks away," said Poppy vaguely. "Would it be okay if she stayed over tonight?"

A tiny furrow appeared on Mrs. Malone's forehead.

"Her mother said it was okay, and I said you wouldn't mind," Poppy added quickly.

Mrs. Malone said, "Well, I really should call her myself. Do you have her number?"

"Um, Nerissa does, but her mother's out running errands right now," Poppy improvised. "She'll be around later this afternoon if you want to talk to her."

"All right. Be sure to remind me," said Mrs. Malone as they went inside, where almost the whole family had gathered in the living room. Will was sprawled on the floor, his eyes closed. Rolly was sitting on the window seat and drumming his heels against the wall with a steady, dull beat. Mr. Malone was slouched in his favorite rocker. Only Franny, who was still with her new friend, Ashley, was missing.

Once Mrs. Malone had introduced everyone to

Nerissa, she perched on one end of the couch, holding a pencil and her small memo pad.

"Now, it's time to address the question at hand," she said in a businesslike way. "Your father and I have decided that the best way to have a close encounter with an alien civilization is to invite them to join us, so we plan to beam a message into the universe as soon as we get back to the houseboat. Naturally, the invitation must be extremely compelling. After all, there are quite a few galaxies in the universe that they might want to visit—"

"One hundred and twenty-five billion, to be exact," said Poppy.

Mrs. Malone paused. "Excuse me, dear?"

"That's how many galaxies there are in the universe," Poppy explained. "One hundred and twenty-five billion. So when you think about it, the odds that they would come to a little planet in a tiny solar system in an out-of-the-way galaxy like ours—well, they're pretty small."

"Exactly my point," said Mrs. Malone. "And all

those galaxies have many, many, many planets, so we must craft a message that really makes them want to come to see us, here on the planet Earth. It's quite a challenge! So, now"—she held out her pencil, poised over the open notebook as if about to jot down a flood of ideas—"if you could send any message to aliens who may be visiting our planet, what would it be?"

"This sounds like the kind of creative homework assignment that Mrs. Gillespie used to give in English class," Will remarked without opening his eyes. "She thought writing about what you did on your summer vacation was damaging to the human spirit, so she kept making us be *creative*." He made a gagging noise.

"Please, Will, we have a guest," said Mrs. Malone. "So, any ideas? Don't be shy. Remember, there's no such thing as a bad—"

"We could ask them to come to dinner," suggested Rolly. "We could give them our address. We could say, please come to 1219 Arden Lane, Austin, Texas, the United States—"

"The Earth, the Milky Way, the Universe," Poppy and Will finished in a chorus.

"Thank you, Rolly," said Mrs. Malone. "That's a very interesting idea indeed. But perhaps we shouldn't be *too* welcoming—"

Rolly stopped drumming his heels long enough to look insulted. "Why not? You said we wanted them to come over."

"Yesss," she replied. "But—"

"And you said that there's no such thing as a bad idea," he went on with relentless logic.

"That's right, I did, but—"

"And you want them to be able to find us," he added.

"In general, yes," said Mrs. Malone. "But, you see—"

"It's not a good idea to ask aliens over for dinner, Rolly," Will cut in. "They might think we're the main course."

"Shh!" Mrs. Malone shot a warning glance at Will. "What Will means is that one must be a little cautious when one meets strangers."

Rolly fixed his small, black eyes on her. "You mean because they might want to take over the world and make all the people do everything they say?"

He did not sound troubled by this. In fact, he sounded as if he approved and might even be willing to lend a hand.

"Er, I think we're getting off course," Mrs. Malone said. "Any other ideas?" She glanced down at Will, who was lying on the floor with his eyes closed. "Will, surely you have a message you'd like to send to our friends from distant galaxies?"

"Sure," he said grumpily. "This is my message: Go home now. Wherever you're from, it's got to be cooler than here."

"Now, dear—"

He opened his eyes and sat up, pushing a damp strand of hair from his forehead. "Well, I'm *hot*," he said peevishly. "Can't we go to a motel for the night? A motel with air-conditioning?"

"No, we can't," said Mr. Malone. "That would

cost money and it's unnecessary. The houseboat is going to be ready tomorrow. Before you know it, we'll be back on the lake, enjoying the cool breezes."

"If we last until tomorrow," muttered Will.

"Nonsense," Mr. Malone said heartily. "Why, this heat is nothing compared to the month I spent camping near Ayers Rock in Australia. Did I ever tell you about the painting of Wandjina—"

"The Sky God?" said Will. "Only about a million times."

"Ah, but Nerissa hasn't heard this yet, and I'm sure she will find this fascinating," Mr. Malone pointed out, turning to her with the delighted expression of someone who has just realized he has a new audience. "You see, the painting is thousands of years old, yet the Sky God looks exactly like an alien wearing a helmet—"

"Yes, dear, we've seen the photos," said Mrs. Malone.

"Perhaps you'd be interested in hearing about the time I spent exploring the Kailasa Temple in

India," Mr. Malone said to Nerissa. "Three days and nights on my hands and knees, measuring every inch in order to draw an accurate floor plan, sweat dripping into my eyes so that I could barely see, and how often do you think I complained of the heat?"

Nerissa looked baffled. "Um, well—"

"Let me guess," said Will. "Never?"

"Never!" said Mr. Malone triumphantly.

Mrs. Malone cleared her throat in a pointed way. "We were discussing what message we wanted to send to an alien race," she said. "Not the heat index. I only have two possibilities here. Surely one of you has a few more bright ideas to contribute. Poppy, what about you?"

"Well, I don't think it's very logical to send a message in English," she said. "Why don't we just beam the value of pi? After all, that's a mathematical constant, which means it would be recognized throughout the universe."

Will snorted. "Really? The aliens take the trouble to get in their spaceship and travel zillions of miles to get here, and what do we say? 'Welcome to Earth. How about a math lesson?'" He shook his head. "Even if they do come in peace, that *alone* will make them attack us."

"I don't see why," said Poppy with some spirit. "The idea is that pi is the same everywhere, so it will be familiar to them. It will make them feel at home."

"You are the only person in the world who thinks math is cozy," said Will.

Poppy gave him a cool look. "I'm just analyzing all the possibilities and coming to a logical conclusion," she said. "You should try it sometime—"

As the debate raged on, Nerissa listened, her eyes moving alertly back and forth like someone watching a tennis match. Finally Mrs. Malone stood up, cleared her throat, and said, "All right, I think we have exhausted our brains for this evening. Let's see, here are the messages we've come up with so far: First, an invitation to dinner at our house with our address helpfully included—"

Mrs. Malone frowned at her list and drew a firm line through that suggestion. "Second, 'Go home now. Wherever you're from, it's got to be cooler than here.'" Her glance moved to Will. "That doesn't make our planet sound like a very attractive place to visit."

"I'm having heatstroke," Will murmured. "It was the best I could do."

"Third: the number pi." Mrs. Malone settled her glasses more firmly on her nose and ran a finger down the list. "Let's see what else we have here . . ." she muttered. "'What took you so long?,' 'Stand still while I get my camera,' 'If you're able to read this, we have one question: Where did you learn English?,' and 'If you'd like to take someone home with you, pick Rolly—he's really no trouble at all.'"

She gave Will a severe look over the top of her glasses. "I wrote that last one down in order to keep a complete record, but I don't think it was very kind, dear. And we certainly won't make any such suggestion to any member of an alien race.

After all, there's no guarantee that they will share our sense of humor."

"I wasn't being funny," muttered Will, but Mrs. Malone had fortunately moved on.

"Well, we obviously still have work to do," she said. "But for now, I think it's time we all went to bed. Poppy, why don't you get the inflatable mattress out of the hall closet and set it up for Nerissa. There are some sheets there, too. . . . Rolly, you need a bath—"

As Rolly staged his usual protest, Poppy caught Nerissa's eye. "Don't judge all mortals by my family," she said. "You'll get a really weird idea of what humans are like. Come on, I'll show you my room."

This took longer than Poppy thought it would, simply because Nerissa was mesmerized by everything in the human world. She walked up and down the stairs three times, stopped to peer closely at every picture on the walls, and, once they got to Poppy's room, stood in the hall for five minutes opening and closing the door.

Once she finally went inside, Nerissa dropped her backpack on the floor and wandered around the room, turning the light switch on and off, walking barefoot on the rug, trailing her fingertips across the top of the dresser, picking up a stapler and turning it over and over in her hands, reaching down to feel the quilt that covered the bed. Finally she made her way to the window, where she stood for fifteen minutes, gripping the windowsill tightly as she stared out at the treetops.

She reached into her backpack. "I have to hang this up," she said, pulling out the blue-and-silver cloak Poppy had seen the night of the bonfire, draped over a tree branch and glittering in the moonlight.

Even in the ordinary glow of an overhead light, the cloak was spellbindingly beautiful.

After several seconds, Poppy realized that she was staring at it with her mouth hanging open. She shut her mouth with a snap and asked, "What is that?"

"It's my cloak," Nerissa said. She held it out

with both hands so that it hung like a curtain. "Every mermaid has one. It's the most precious thing we own. I need to hang it up so it doesn't get crumpled."

"Yes," Poppy said. The folds of the cloak swayed in front of her eyes, making her feel light-headed. As if in a dream, she reached out to touch it—

"Stop!"

Startled, Poppy stepped back, her hand dropping to her side.

"You can't touch this," Nerisa said fiercely. "Not ever."

"I'm sorry," Poppy stammered. "It's just so . . . amazing. I didn't mean anything . . . here." She opened the closet door. There was a hook on the inside where she could hang her bathrobe, except that she never bothered to do so. "You can put it there," she said.

Nerissa smoothed it out with one hand, then hung it carefully on the hook. She stepped back and tilted her head, looking in the closet at Poppy's shirts, dresses, and skirts hung up in neat rows.

"How many clothes do you have?" asked Nerissa. She sounded curious and a little bewildered, like an explorer who is encountering the strange customs of a remote tribe for the first time.

"Just the normal amount," Poppy said, a little defensively. "I wear T-shirts and shorts when I'm not in school. At my last school, we had to wear khaki pants and polo shirts all the time. And I have a few dresses for when we get to go out to eat or something." She glanced at Nerissa.

"Where did you get those clothes you're wearing?" she asked.

"Oh, it's not hard to find things you need at the lake," said Nerissa. She had moved to a lamp and was turning it on and off, her head tilted to one side as she watched the light with fascination. "People are always losing things or leaving them behind—shoes, sunglasses, swimming goggles."

She turned to the mirror. "That's how I got these," she added with some satisfaction, gesturing toward her shell necklace.

Poppy picked up her notebook and a pencil. "That's interesting," she said in an encouraging tone, jotting down a note. "So how long have you lived in the lake—"

Before she could finish, there was a brisk knock and, without waiting for an invitation, Franny opened the door and stuck her head in.

"Mom told me to remind you that there are extra pillows in the closet for your friend, if you need them." She glanced at Nerissa. "Hi, it's nice to meet—oh!"

Her eyes widened as she spotted the cloak hanging on the door. "Is that yours? It's gorgeous!"

Before Nerissa could answer, Franny walked across the room with a dazed look on her face.

That must have been what I looked like, Poppy thought uneasily. Like I was hypnotized or something . . .

"That's so beautiful," Franny sighed, reaching out to stroke it.

"Don't!" Nerissa shouted.

But Franny, unlike Poppy, didn't stop. She

didn't even seem to hear Nerissa. She was just about to touch the cloak when Nerissa grabbed her arm and pulled her away.

Franny jerked out of Nerissa's grasp and glared at her. "What are you doing?" she snapped. "I wasn't going to hurt anything."

Poppy held her breath. She knew what Franny was like when she was annoyed and she had a feeling, from the little she knew of Nerissa, that she might have a temper as well. Still, at least Franny's face had lost that awful zombie expression.

"You can't touch it," Nerissa said. "It's mine."

"I got that, thanks," Franny said coldly. She flipped her hair back and said pointedly to Poppy, "I'm glad that *my* new friend is someone like Ashley, who doesn't mind sharing things."

Then she turned on her heel and left in a huff.

"Don't mind her," Poppy said. "She's thirteen. It's turned her brain."

Nerissa shrugged. "That's okay. She reminds me a little bit of Kali and Ariadne."

Poppy grinned. "You're right," she said. "In

fact, the three of them would probably get along really well."

And for the first time, Poppy heard Nerissa giggle.

Poppy couldn't wait to ask Nerissa questions about being a mermaid, but it was hard to get her to focus—there were so many things that Nerissa found odd, strange, or interesting about the way people lived. She spent fifteen minutes pulling curtains open and closed and another half hour turning the bathroom faucet on and off. She walked back and forth on Poppy's rug a dozen times, wiggling her toes on the rug and murmuring under her breath in wonderment.

"And I haven't even turned on the TV or stereo yet," said Poppy.

"What?" Nerissa looked up, her eyes glazed over.

"Nothing. We need to save some excitement for tomorrow," Poppy said.

Finally Poppy got her to agree to sit down long

enough to trade answers. For every question Poppy answered, Nerissa had to answer one of hers in return.

They both took careful notes. Poppy found out that some mermaids swim around the world, following ocean currents from the icy waters of the Arctic to the tropical warmth of the South Sea, but that most find a watery home where they feel comfortable and stay there for centuries.

She learned that mermaids who settled in lakes often had ongoing feuds with the water nymphs who lived in rivers or ponds (mermaids thought the nymphs were silly and nymphs claimed the mermaids were stuck-up).

"And we eat algae," Nerissa said in a challenging voice. "I suppose you think that's disgusting."

"Not at all," said Poppy unconvincingly. "I've read that spirulina actually has lots of vitamins. And I've eaten seaweed at a sushi restaurant before."

They were still talking at ten o'clock, when

Mrs. Malone knocked on the door and poked her head in. "Lights out, girls," she said. "We're getting up early tomorrow to go to the lake. The mechanic called and said that the boat's been fixed."

"Really?" Poppy sat up straighter. "Hey, Mom, can Nerissa come with us?"

"Well, I don't know . . . I'd have to ask her mother. . . ." Mrs. Malone said.

"She'll say yes," said Nerissa quickly. "I know she will."

"Please, Mom?" Poppy rarely resorted to pleading with her parents, but this was a special case. "It's not fair that Will's hanging out with Henry and Franny's spending so much time with Ashley, and I'm stuck by myself."

"You could always spend time with Rolly," said Mrs. Malone. "You would be a good influence on him. Maybe you could encourage him to stop storing his bait in the fridge—"

Poppy groaned. "Mom!"

Mrs. Malone's gaze moved to Nerissa. "Well, it's fine with me," she said, "if it's all right with

Nerissa's mom." As she drifted out of the room, she added vaguely, "Oh dear, I have so much to do, my list is huge! . . . remind me to call her tomorrow . . . good night . . ."

Chapter
TEN

When the Malones arrived at the marina the next morning, things did not go as planned.

They found a crowd of people clustered at the end of the dock. There was the sound of joking and laughter and a hum of interest and excitement. Above the heads of the crowd, they could see a huge sign that read, "World-famous Mermaid Show!"

"What," asked Nerissa in a terrible voice, "is *that*?"

"I don't know. Come on, let's check it out," said Poppy, pushing her way through the crowd.

A large, jolly-looking man stood next to a table that had a huge TV monitor on it. He was chatting with the bystanders.

"I'm Bud," he told them. "Bud McCray. And you folks are in for a treat this weekend. See that restaurant over there? Well, they hired me to bring my world-famous mermaids here for a special performance. They came all the way from Galveston to put on a show."

"Galveston?" said Nerissa under her breath. "I've met the Galveston mermaids. They wear seaweed in their hair and strings of barnacles around their necks. Coralie calls them barbarians. They don't *perform* for people; they try to *eat* them."

"Shh," Poppy whispered. "Listen."

"That's their home, you see," he said genially. "They've lived there for hundreds of years, frolicking by the seawall. Then in 1932, Horace Abner Tate happened to go for an early morning fishing expedition and caught sight of them. Well, the mermaids were shy, of course, and swam away as soon as they saw him. But he kept coming back. After a while, he earned their trust and, being a savvy businessman, he pitched them the idea of doing a show. It took a bit of convincing, but the mermaids finally came around. Horace hired a choreographer to teach them a water ballet—and the rest is history!"

The grown-ups in the crowd laughed. Nerissa scowled.

"This can't be true," she hissed in Poppy's ear. "No real mermaid would ever lower herself to provide entertainment for mortals!"

"Of course it's not true," Poppy whispered back. "It's just a stunt."

"What's the best place to watch the show?" one of the onlookers asked.

"You can get a great view from the restaurant's outdoor deck," Bud McCray said. "But if you really want an up-close and personal look at the mermaids, I'd recommend you buy a ticket to go out on the lake in one of our glass-bottom boats. We're bringing in a whole fleet of boats, just for this show. And take a look at this! We've even managed to set up a live feed to the mermaids' underwater home—"

He turned on a laptop that was connected to the TV monitor. Two women appeared on the screen.

They seemed to be floating underwater, waving cheerfully and smiling dazzling white smiles. One woman wore a blue bikini top. Her legs seemed to be wrapped in matching blue cloth that ended in a fish tail. The other woman wore the same costume, except in green.

"May I introduce Mermaid Crystal"—he waved to the woman in blue, who tilted her head saucily to one side—"and Mermaid Shannon"—he pointed toward the woman wearing green, who winked. "You will be astonished by their ability to drink a soda, play a game of football, and hold a tea party— all underwater! You will be beguiled by their charm, their beauty, and their amazing swimming abilities! Watch as they live their lives underwater, doing everything from playing a game of touch football to presenting a tribute to America!"

The crowd laughed. Bud McCray opened a box of brochures and started handing them out.

"Football! Tea parties!" Nerissa was fuming.

"Shh," said Poppy. "People are looking."

A little girl tugged at the woman's hand. "I want

to see the mermaids, Mommy!" she said. "Please?"

The woman laughed and shrugged. "Looks like you've sold two tickets already," she said, handing over the money.

Bud McCray grinned as he gave her the tickets. "You'll have a great time, I guarantee," he said. Then he leaned down to look the little girl in the eye. "And you, little lady, will be one of the very few people who have ever seen a real live mermaid! You'll be telling your grandchildren about this!"

A ripple of laughter ran through the crowd. Everybody knew it was a hoax, Poppy thought. Everybody was in on the joke,

Everybody except the little girl—and Nerissa.

Before Poppy could stop her, Nerissa stomped up to Bud McCray, grabbed one of the brochures, crumpled it up, and waved it under his nose.

"This is wrong," she said angrily. "You are exploiting mermaids by making fun of them in this way."

Bud looked confused, but he quickly recovered. "You're not one of those activists, are you?" he asked.

"A what?" asked Nerissa.

"You're not going to start protesting for mermaid rights, now, are you?" he said, chuckling. "Because I tell you what, picket lines really mess up our business."

It was clear that Nerissa didn't understand, but she bristled all the same. Poppy tried to shoot her a warning look, but Nerissa was too angry to catch it.

"Why shouldn't mermaids have rights?" she demanded. "They shouldn't be forced to perform tricks to amuse people. It's . . . it's undignified."

Bud McCray started laughing. He laughed so hard that tears actually ran down his cheeks. (Poppy had often read about this in books and was fascinated to see it happen in real life. What books didn't tell you was that a person who was laughing that hard usually snorted a bit, which was not attractive at all. Books also didn't say how annoying the laugh would sound if the person was laughing at you.)

"Listen, honey, I'll tell you a little secret," he

finally said when he had calmed down. He leaned over and whispered, "These aren't real mermaids! They're just women who are real good at swimming and breathing air through a little rubber tube. We dress 'em up like mermaids and they put on a little show and smile at the customers and everybody's happy."

Nerissa's eyes still glinted. "That's no better than capturing real mermaids and making them do your bidding," she said. "In fact, that's even more horrible."

Now it was Bud's turn to look confused. "What's horrible?"

"Pretending that they're really mermaids!" Nerissa said impatiently. "Real mermaids were surfing the Gulf Stream and diving to the ocean depths when mortals were still living in caves! They can call the wind and make waves do their bidding! They are mentioned in ancient myths and age-old folklore! They are not"—she paused to glare at the man—"a *sideshow act*."

Bud McCray stopped smiling and began to look

annoyed. "Is this a prank?" he asked Poppy. "Did someone put you up to this?"

"N-no, of course not," Poppy stammered.

"Because I happen to know that Dutch Owens wanted to get this gig," he continued, squinting at them suspiciously. "He has Ralphie the Diving Pig, you know, and it just eats him up that my mermaids are more popular than his pig. He never had a chance to land this contract and he knows it! I wouldn't put it past him to send you two in just to mess with me."

"I don't know Dutch or Ralphie," said Poppy. "My friend is just quite passionate about, um, issues of social justice."

"I'll say." Bud snorted. He glared at Nerissa. "If you ask me, you're a little too old to believe in mermaids. Now, I have some paying customers to attend to."

He turned away from them, ready to sell more tickets. Poppy saw Nerissa's scowl deepen, then felt the hot, breathless day change in a moment. A wind picked up, frothing the water on the lake and making the sign for the mermaid show twist and rattle in the air.

"Nerissa, stop it!" Poppy hissed.

Nerissa didn't even turn her head. She stared up at the gathering clouds, her eyes narrowed.

"Nerissa!" Poppy pulled on her arm. "We won't get to have any fun on the houseboat if you call up a storm."

For a moment, Poppy didn't think Nerissa was even listening, but then she saw her shoulders relax and she nodded. The wind died down and the clouds vanished, leaving a sky so blue that it dazzled Poppy's eyes.

"Thanks," Poppy said. "Come on, let's get on board. I can't wait to show you the waterslide!"

Two hours later, Nerissa seemed to have forgotten the mermaid show. She and Poppy had competed with Will and Henry to see who could make the biggest splash on the waterslide. Then Franny had joined them and Nerissa had dazzled everyone with her ability to dive deep into the lake, then swim quickly toward the surface and launch herself into the air.

After lunch, Mr. and Mrs. Malone (who had been up until three a.m. looking through the telescope for UFOs) decided to take a nap. They even managed to convince a yawning Rolly to take one as well. Poppy, Nerissa, and Franny stretched out on lounge chairs while Will and Henry had second helpings.

"I think I'll live on a houseboat when I grow up," said Will, munching on the last of the potato chips. "This is pretty sweet."

"You'll have to make a lot of money," Poppy pointed out. "If you want a boat like this, at least."

"No problem." He waved his hand in the air, scattering potato chip crumbs. "I'll just be a paranormal investigator."

"Ha," said Franny. "Like Mom and Dad?"

"No, like Oliver Asquith," said Will. "I plan to be a globe-trotting celebrity with my own TV show. That way, someone else will rent the cool houseboat and I'll get to live on it."

"Good luck with that," said Franny, standing up. "I'm going to take a shower. Dibs on the bathroom."

Will rolled his eyes. "Haven't you been in the water enough today?" he asked. "Why do you always want to get cleaned up if you don't have to?"

"You may want to live like a savage," sniffed Franny, "but I prefer to be civilized. Even if I don't have to."

She stalked off to go belowdecks. Poppy and Nerissa hung out with Will and Henry for a little while, then went to their bunks to change out of their bathing suits.

Poppy was pulling a T-shirt over her head when she heard Nerissa say, "Hey."

There was something in her tone of voice that made Poppy's stomach clench. Quickly, she pulled the shirt down. Nerissa's face was white with shock.

"What's wrong?" asked Poppy.

"Where's my cloak?" Nerissa sounded on the edge of panic. "I hung it on the back of the door, and it's not here!"

"Maybe it fell down," Poppy said. "Did you look around the bed?"

"Of course I did! That took about ten seconds," Nerissa said, waving a hand at the tiny bunk. "It's gone."

"Don't worry," said Poppy. "I'm sure it's here somewhere. . . ."

She bit her lip and glanced around the cabin. There was barely enough room for a bunk. Poppy picked up the pillow on the bed, without much hope that she would find anything.

She was right. There was nothing there.

"I can't lose that cloak!" Nerissa's voice was even higher. "This is a disaster!"

Panic, Poppy discovered, could be catching. Her heart was starting to beat a little faster.

"Okay, let's just stay calm," she began, but she was interrupted by the sound of loud knocking.

"Franny!" Will yelled. "Quit hogging the bathroom!"

He pounded on the door again.

"I'm sure it's not lost." Poppy spoke more loudly

to be heard over the racket. "It's just . . . momentarily misplaced."

Nerissa's lip trembled. "I've got to find it," she said in a small voice. "If I don't—"

"Franny!" It was Will again. "Are you trying to set a world record for the longest shower ever?"

"Oh, for heaven's sake." Poppy jerked open the door and went out to where Will was standing, glaring at the bathroom door. Henry was leaning against the wall, watching him with amusement.

"Would you be quiet?" Poppy snapped. "Nerissa's upset and your yelling isn't making things any better."

"How much time can a person spend in a shower that's so small you knock your elbow on the wall when you reach for the soap?" Will asked. He pounded on the door again. "Franny!"

"Here, let me try." Poppy leaned closer to the door and said loudly, "Franny, I just saw Colt go by on a Jet Ski! Don't you want to be on deck when he circles back around?"

Will grinned. "Brilliant!" he whispered. "Stand back. Don't let the door hit you when she stampedes out of there."

But the door remained closed.

"Aggh." Will leaned against the wall and slid down to the floor.

"Dude, I didn't know you cared so much about hygiene." Henry smirked.

Will folded his arms and gave Henry an icy stare. "Look, I don't care about washing my hands before dinner, but my mother has this fixation—"

"Shh." Poppy held up a hand, then put her ear to the door. "Listen."

"What?" Will said grumpily, but he scooted over and put his ear to the door, too.

For a moment, there was silence. Then came the sound of a whimper.

"Franny? Are you all right?" Poppy asked.

There was a pause, then Franny said, "No . . ." Her voice wobbled as if she were crying.

"What's wrong?"

"I can't tell you! It's too horrible."

"What, did you run out of conditioner or some-thing?" grumbled Will.

"No!" Franny's voice trembled on the edge of hysteria. "It's worse than that! Much, much worse!"

"Can you open the door?" Henry asked.

"No!"

"Should we get Mom and Dad?" Poppy suggested.

"No!" Franny wailed. "They can't see me! Nobody can!"

"Come on, Franny, we can't help you if you won't open the door," Poppy said. "Whatever's happened, I'm sure it's not as bad as you think."

"It is, it is," Franny wept. "You have no idea. How could you? Nothing like this has ever hap-pened to anyone, ever! I've turned into a freak!"

Will rolled his eyes at Poppy. "I bet she tried to dye her hair again," he whispered. "I bet it's purple this time."

"Shh." Poppy turned back to the door. "Listen. Whatever's happened, I'm sure we can help you, but only if you let us in. . . ."

Poppy had experience in talking Franny down when she was about to have hysterics. The longest this had ever taken her was six minutes, twelve seconds (Poppy had started recording the times in her logbook, on the chance that she might want to write a case study about Franny someday, perhaps for a journal that focused on psychologically unstable personalities). This time, however, it took Poppy a full fifteen minutes to convince her sister to open the door a tiny crack. She only agreed to do this if Poppy promised to not let anyone else look inside.

"Fine. I promise," said Poppy, exasperated.

The door creaked open an inch.

Poppy gave it a push, just enough to stick her head in, and said, "So what's all the fuss—oh no! What happened?"

"That's what I've been trying to tell you," Franny said tearfully. "I don't know!"

"What's going on?" Ignoring Franny's protests, Will pushed the door open even wider and looked in.

Then he, too, stood still, staring, with his mouth hanging open.

Franny was sitting on the floor, half in and half out of the shower. Water was still spraying over her, turning her long blond curls into limp rats tails.

But that wasn't what had Poppy and Will rooted to the spot with horror.

Franny's legs were gone. In their place was a long tail with glittering blue scales.

Chapter
ELEVEN

erissa was furious. "I told you not to touch that!" she yelled at Franny. "Now look what you've done!"

"I just wanted to try it on," Franny said, her eyes wide and pleading. "I was going to put it right back—"

"Well, it's too late for that now," Nerissa snapped. "Thanks to you, I'll never be able to go home again! I'll have to stay a mortal forever!"

Will and Henry looked from Franny to Nerissa, astonished.

"What happened to Franny?" Henry asked Poppy.

"What do you mean, you'll have to stay a mortal?" Will asked Nerissa.

They were both ignored.

"I thought you didn't want to go back," Poppy said to Nerissa. "I thought you were running away."

"I was!" Nerissa cried. "But not for the rest of my life! I only wanted to be human for a day or two, then I was going to turn back into a mermaid! That was the plan. And now she"—she scowled ferociously at Franny—"has ruined everything."

"I didn't mean to!" Franny wailed. "And now I'm, I'm—" She stared down at the scales covering what used to be her legs and burst into loud sobs. "I've turned into a fish!"

"Mermaid," Nerissa said frostily.

"Wait a second," said Will, clutching his head. "Nerissa's really a mermaid? And now Franny's one, too?"

"Exactly," said Poppy, exasperated. "Try to keep up, Will." She turned to Franny, who was still sobbing, and hissed, "Be quiet! Do you want Mom and Dad to hear you?"

Will and Henry exchanged an uncomfortable look.

"Come on, Franny," Will said. "If you keep this up, you'll turn Lake Travis into a saltwater lake."

This only made Franny sob even harder. Will rolled his eyes. Henry sighed. Nerissa said something under her breath that Poppy was glad she couldn't hear.

"Okay, everybody take a deep breath," said Poppy. "Let's think this through. Nerissa, what do we have to do to turn her back?"

"How should I know?" Nerissa said. "I've never heard of a mortal who was silly enough to try on a mermaid's cloak—"

"Well, who expects to put on a cloak and turn into a mermaid?" snapped Franny, who stopped crying long enough to glare at Nerissa. "That would be like, like . . . putting on a fur coat and turning into a bear!"

"It's not at all the same thing—" Nerissa began.

But at that moment, Franny suddenly turned pale and fell back onto the linoleum. She moaned slightly as her eyelids closed.

"Franny?" Poppy grabbed her hand. It was cold

and clammy. She looked over her shoulder at Nerissa. "What's going on? What's wrong with her?"

Nerissa frowned. "I think she's having the same kind of reaction any mermaid would have if she spends more than an hour out of the water."

"It looks like she's gone into shock," said Will. "What should we do?"

"We have to get her into the lake, fast," said Nerissa.

Poppy straightened up. "We'd better call Mom and Dad—"

"No!" Nerissa almost shouted.

They turned to stare at her.

"You can't do that," she said. "No one can know that mermaids exist. There have been a few times in our history when humans have found out where we lived." She added darkly, "It's always ended badly."

Poppy frowned. Ended badly for whom? she thought. The mermaids . . . or the mortals?

"But Poppy's right," said Henry. "We need to get help."

"If you tell your parents," Nerissa said quickly, "I won't help you figure out how to turn Franny back into a mortal."

"We don't need your help," Will said. "Anyway, you said you didn't know what to do, either."

"I don't," Nerissa admitted. "But Coralie might."

Will threw his hands up. "Okay," he said. "Who's Coralie?"

"Shh." Poppy cast a worried glance over her shoulder. "She's like, I don't know . . . the head of the mermaids."

"Oh, right, of course." Will nodded several times. "I suppose she's a sort of queen? Runs the mermaid crew? Makes sure that everyone stays together when they go out for a swim?"

"We are not called a crew," said Nerissa coldly. "The proper term of a group of mermaids is a mischief. And Coralie has been our monarch for the last five centuries. If anyone knows what to do in this situation, it's her. We should get Franny in the lake, then take her to the cove to ask Coralie for help."

Poppy and Will glanced at each other.

"Your parents won't know what to do; you know they won't," said Nerissa. "And Coralie won't help any mortal—unless I ask her to."

Poppy looked at Franny. Her skin was so white that Poppy could see the blue vein in her wrist throbbing. Was it her imagination, or was Franny's pulse getting more faint?

"She doesn't have much time," Nerissa said urgently.

"Okay," Poppy said. "Will and Henry, you grab Franny's shoulders. Nerissa and I will take her tail. . . ."

The tail was much heavier than Poppy thought it would be and more slippery, too. It didn't help that four people had to squeeze into a tiny bathroom and work together to pick Franny up. Finally, however, after whispered arguments about who was getting in whose way, they managed to stagger onto the deck with Franny between them.

Perhaps it was the fresh air that revived her.

Franny's eyes fluttered open again just as they reached the railing.

"On the count of three," said Poppy.

"Wait!" Franny yelled. "What are you doing?"

"One—"

"My hair!"

"Two—"

"My mascara!"

"Three!"

And with a mighty effort, they threw Franny overboard.

Chapter
TWELVE

"Where is she?" Poppy leaned over the railing as far as she dared. "Do you see her?"

"No," said Will, looking worried.

"Neither do I," Henry said.

"Is she at the bottom of the lake, do you think?" Nerissa asked. "She sank like a stone, she did." She bit her lip. "If she drowns, I'll never be able to go back—"

"Stop thinking about yourself for one second!" Poppy turned on her, furious. "I thought you said this was the only thing we could do to save her."

"It was," Nerissa said. "She would have died if she didn't get into water soon. But you didn't tell me she couldn't swim."

"She can," said Will, peering anxiously into the lake. "We all took lessons when we lived in Coral Gables. But she never goes in the water—"

"She says the chlorine in swimming pools dries her hair out," said Poppy. She paled, struck by a terrible thought. "You don't suppose she *forgot* how to swim, do you?"

"I don't think that's possible," Henry said. "Isn't it like riding a bike? Something people never forget?"

Will shielded his eyes with his hands and scanned the lake. "Of course, if anyone could do an idiotic thing like forgetting how to swim, it's Franny—"

He was interrupted by what looked like a giant fish shooting up out of the lake, then landing back in the water with a slap of its tail that sprayed water over Will and Poppy.

"What was that?" Will sputtered.

Poppy dashed water out of her eyes and squinted. "I'm not sure—"

At that moment, Franny's head popped up

above the still surface of the lake. Her skin was rosy once more, her eyes bright. She smiled up to them and gave a little wave.

"Sorry I got you wet," she said breezily. "But did you see me? Wasn't that *great*?"

"Franny, you scared us!" Poppy glanced over her shoulder, then lowered her voice. "We thought you'd drowned!"

"Me? Drown?" Franny laughed. "That's impossible! Watch this. . . ."

She dove under the water. A few seconds later, she vaulted up into the air, turned a somersault, and splashed down again. "See? I look amazing, don't I?"

"Stop showing off!" said Will. "Do you want Mom and Dad to see you?"

"Oh, don't be such a spoilsport," said Franny, flicking a strand of wet hair away from her face. "I'm just having a little fun. And I can't believe how . . . powerful I feel!"

Poppy and Will glanced at each other. They felt a little unnerved by this. Franny had always seemed scatterbrained, vain, and (in her worse moments) a little ditzy. That could be annoying at times—most of the time, if Poppy was honest with herself—but at least they knew what to expect. This Franny, the Franny who sounded strong and confident and bold, was brand-new. Poppy wasn't sure what to make of her.

"I'm going to swim all the way to the other side of the lake," Franny called out.

Henry's eyes widened. "You can't! That's miles away."

"Who cares?" She shot off.

Nerissa made a little sound. Poppy turned to her and saw that she was staring after Franny with a strange, intense look on her face.

In only a few minutes, Franny circled back to the boat, laughing with delight.

"Did you see that?" she called. "Now I'm going to swim to the *other* side!" She sped away again.

Nerissa's eyebrows drew together and her lips tightened. Watching her, Poppy shivered, then glanced at the sky.

A cloud had moved in front of the sun, casting a shadow over the lake.

The shadow was what made me shiver, she thought. That's all.

"It's not right," Nerissa said under her breath. "I'm a mermaid, not her."

"But you don't like being a mermaid, remember?" said Poppy. "If you hadn't decided to try being a human, none of this would have happened."

"Your sister stole my cloak!" Nerissa snapped, her voice rising. "If she hadn't done *that*, everything would be fine."

The cloud darkened. A breeze sprang up, bringing with it a smell of rain and kicking up little waves on the surface of the lake.

"Okay, she shouldn't have done that," Poppy admitted. "But she wouldn't have had the chance if you hadn't decided to run away from your family."

Nerissa's eyes narrowed dangerously. "This isn't my fault," she said, spacing each word apart for added emphasis.

A few seconds later, fat drops began to fall. The waves got bigger and choppier.

Poppy clenched her hands. She wanted to argue with Nerissa, wanted to say that it was at least partly her fault, but she also didn't want them to have to deal with a raging thunderstorm at the same time they were trying to help Franny.

"You're right, it isn't," she said peaceably. "It's entirely Franny's fault. She was very wrong to take your cloak. On behalf of my sister, I apologize."

Nerissa looked at Poppy for a long moment, then nodded. "I accept the apology," she said grandly. "On behalf of your sister, who is very lucky to have you around."

The wind died down. The rain stopped. The cloud disappeared. Once more, the day was hot and sunny, and the lake was calm.

Poppy sighed with relief. Just then, Franny swam back into view. She floated in the water below them, smiling up at them with delight. "This is amazing! I bet I could swim a circuit of the lake before you even get the kayaks in the water."

Nerissa leaned over the railing and scowled at Franny. "Don't go anywhere! You don't know anything about being a mermaid. You'll get lost or someone will see you and capture you or you'll get hit by a powerboat—"

Franny's laughter floated across the water. "I'll be fine," she said gaily. "You all worry too much!"

"Nerissa's right," Poppy called. "Wait for us. . . ."

They rushed to the kayaks but, as always, it took longer than they thought it would to put on their life jackets and lower the kayaks over the side of the houseboat. Franny watched for a while, but soon became bored. She began diving under the water and leaping up out of the air, sometimes doing flips and sometimes trying new tricks, like half-twists and double somersaults.

After one particularly ambitious triple gainer, Rolly's head popped out of the galley door.

"What was that?" he asked, his eyes glittering with excitement.

Poppy turned to face him, her back to the

railing, hoping that she was blocking his view of Franny.

"What was what?" she asked innocently.

"That splash." Rolly trotted over to the railing. "Was it Mugwump? Because it sounded like Mugwump."

"Of course it wasn't," Poppy said. "It was just a fish."

Nerissa nodded. "A regular, ordinary fish."

"And small," Will added.

"That's right," said Henry. "A very small, very ordinary fish."

Rolly frowned. "It didn't sound small," he said. "It sounded huge. It sounded like a whale."

Will snickered. Behind her, Poppy could hear Franny's squeak of outrage.

Rolly stood still for a moment, his lips pressed tight in thought. "I'm getting my fishing pole," he said, marching back belowdecks.

"Quick!" Poppy said to the others. "We have to get away from here before Rolly sees something or before he wakes up Mom and Dad."

Henry and Will were grunting with the effort of lowering their kayak.

"Hold on," Henry said. "Lower the bow first—"

"I'm trying! Give me a second!" Will said.

With a splash, the kayak landed in the water. Will and Henry got in. Poppy and Nerissa managed to get the other double kayak in the water just as Mr. and Mrs. Malone came up on the deck. Mrs. Malone was wearing a shockingly pink canvas sun hat and a huge pair of sunglasses. Mr. Malone's nose was white from the zinc oxide he had rubbed on it; he was carrying the telescope and tripod.

"Where are you kids going?" he called out. "We've got work to do."

"We're going to that little cove over there," Poppy yelled back. "Franny said that Ashley said that her father said that one of his friends told him he had heard from someone that there was a strange glow in the sky last week. He took a picture. It looked like the glow was hovering right over the cove."

"Really!" Mr. Malone halted, his face bright

with interest. "That sounds like an excellent lead."

"Exactly," Will put in hastily. "And we want to follow it on our own, because—"

He hesitated and cast a wild look at Poppy.

"Because it's time we tested our investigation skills," she finished smoothly. "After all, we're going to go into the family business someday, right?"

Mr. and Mrs. Malone both stopped. Mr. Malone carefully set the tripod and telescope down on the deck. They looked at Poppy and Will for a moment, then turned to smile at each other. Even from a distance, Poppy could tell their eyes were getting misty.

"Oh, great," Will muttered. "They're about to have a 'I'm-So-Very-Proud-of-You' moment."

"Oh, Emerson!" said Mrs. Malone in a trembling voice.

"I know, Lucille," Mr. Malone managed to choke out. "I know."

Will sighed loudly. "We're taking off now, all right?" he yelled. "See you later!"

"Wait!" Mr. Malone stepped to the railing. "Before you go, I wanted to tell you"—he paused, blinking, to clear his throat—"well, just hearing that you all want to follow in our footsteps . . . it's every parent's dream. . . ."

He choked up again.

"There, there, dear." Mrs. Malone patted his arm, then smiled tearfully at Poppy and Will. "Your father and I are"—she took a deep breath—"we are So Very Proud of You! We can't wait to hear about the first paranormal discovery you make on your very own!"

Chapter
THIRTEEN

"**I** wonder what Mom and Dad would say about this discovery," muttered Will as Franny shot up out of the water and did a somersault over their kayaks, landing with a giant splash.

"Aggh—Franny, stop it!" said Poppy, wiping water off her face. "I don't think they would be too pleased, actually."

"I don't know," said Henry. "Maybe they'd like having a mermaid in the family. They could study her close to home."

"All the more reason why we can't tell them," said Poppy.

Franny popped up on the other side of Poppy's kayak. "Hey, guess what?" she said. "I can breathe underwater!"

"Yeah, that's great, Franny," said Poppy, distracted. "Nerissa, are you sure we'll find Coralie at the cove—"

She glanced over her shoulder at Nerissa and saw a stricken expression on her face.

"I don't think you have to worry about finding the others," Nerissa said. "I think *they've* found *us*."

Franny stopped swimming. "Others?" she asked. "What others?"

Suddenly, there was a swirl of water and three mermaids appeared. They were smiling strange smiles at Franny as they slowly swam around the two kayaks.

Poppy recognized them. There was the blond girl, the one who had reminded her of Franny—what was her name? Oh, yes. Ariadne.

And there was the girl with the spiky black hair and pointed chin. Poppy remembered her name, too. Kali.

And the older woman with silver hair . . .

"Hi, Coralie," said Nerissa in a subdued voice.

"Nerissssssa," said Coralie, drawing out the name with a hiss. She swam closer. Franny moved her arms in the water, trying to back away, and bumped into Ariadne.

"Don't worry," the blond girl crooned. "We won't hurt you. We just didn't know there were any other mermaids in the lake, that's all."

Franny gulped. "I—I'm not really a mermaid," she whispered.

The other girl laughed. "You didn't have to tell us that," she said. "Your skin is too pink and your eyes are too warm. In fact, I'd think you were human if it weren't for—"

"That tail," said Ariadne. "Although it does look rather familiar. . . ."

She dove under the water, then reemerged on the other side of Franny. She shook her head, drops of water scattering in the sun, and directed a cold smile at Nerissa.

"Why, it looks a bit like Nerissa's tail," she said innocently. "How could that be?"

Kali dove down as well, then emerged from the water on the other side of Poppy's kayak, laughing. "And Nerissa has what look like"—she tried to stifle her giggles and failed—"human legs!"

Ariadne's mocking laughter joined Kali's. Nerisssa blushed.

Coralie narrowed her eyes. "Now, then," she said. "What is this all about?"

Poppy couldn't help feeling sorry for Nerissa. Apparently, letting one's cloak out of one's possession was one of the worst things a mermaid could do. When Nerissa confessed that she had stuffed her cloak in a backpack and gone off to spend time with mortals, her voice barely rose above a whisper.

"How could you be so careless!" said Coralie. "It's bad enough that you had to run away and try being human. Still, everyone gets a little restless when they're young; everyone wants to take a few risks. But to let your cloak out of your sight and then to have it stolen by a mortal—"

"I. Didn't. Steal. It," said Franny. "I just tried it on."

Coralie tilted her head to one side and looked closely at Franny. "You knew it wasn't yours, did you not? And I'm sure Nerissa told you not to touch it."

"Well, yes." Franny bit her lip and looked embarrassed. "But I couldn't help it! It was so beautiful. . . ."

Her voice trailed off. For a long moment, there was nothing but silence.

Then Coralie smiled.

Poppy's heart seemed to skip a beat. Coralie's smile was warm and friendly and forgiving. It should have made Poppy feel better, but it didn't. Instead, it made alarm bells go off in her head.

"Of course, my dear. I quite understand." Coralie's voice had changed, too. It was as warm and melting and sweet as honey on hot toast. "The temptation must have been impossible to resist— especially since the color looks simply stunning with your eyes."

For the first time since the mermaids had arrived, a slight smile appeared on Franny's face. "It does?"

"Absolutely!" said Ariadne. She swam over to Franny. "And your hair is lovely," she added. "Almost as nice as mine."

She lifted a strand of her own hair, then dropped it. It fell to her shoulder in a perfect curl.

Franny gulped. "Th-thank you," she said. "Ho-how do you keep your hair looking so great? I mean, if you're in the water all the time—"

Ariadne cast her eyes down, as if embarrassed by the compliment, but Poppy could see her sly smile. "I'll show you if you like," Ariadne said. "You will see. Your hair will be the envy of every mortal."

"That would be great!" said Franny, beaming. "Thank you so so so much!"

Poppy frowned. Why were Coralie and Ariadne being so nice all of a sudden? The alarm bells got louder.

"Er, Franny, listen," said Poppy. "I'm not sure that's a good idea—"

She was interrupted by a Jet Ski zooming by. Poppy caught a glimpse of Colt's white-blond hair, then the Jet Ski slipped in between two sailboats and was gone. She turned to see Franny sighing and gazing wistfully after the Jet Ski.

Kali's sharp eyes had noticed it, too.

"Do you know that person?" she asked Franny. "Do you like him?"

Franny blushed. "No, of course not," she said, too quickly. "I mean, I do know him, his name is Colt, he's my friend Ashley's brother, but I'm not interested in him at all. . . ."

Ariadne met Kali's eyes. They both smirked.

"Oh, that's too bad," Kali said, "Because if you did like him—"

"We could show you how to make him notice you," said Ariadne.

Franny hesitated. "Really?"

"Don't listen to them, Franny," said Nerissa.

Poppy twisted around in her seat. From the look on Nerissa's face, she was hearing the same alarm bells as Poppy.

"Why not?" Franny swam closer to Ariadne and Kali. "They're just being nice."

"Nice!" said Nerissa in disgust. "Mermaids aren't nice. And we're not friendly or helpful or kind, either. Those two are up to something."

But Franny wasn't listening.

"Try turning your head like this," suggested Ariadne, tilting her head and glancing up from under her eyelashes. "Then look like this"—a teasing smile appeared on her lips—"and then wave like this. . . ."

She fluttered her fingers in the air.

Franny copied her exactly.

"Perfect," said Kali, her eyes gleaming with mischief. "Before you know it, you'll have boys jumping off their boats to be with you."

"Oh, yuck," muttered Will.

"How long do we have to listen to all this girl stuff?" asked Henry, making a face.

Coralie raised an eyebrow. "Girl stuff?" she repeated, outraged. "May I remind you that we are *mermaids*?"

Will rolled his eyes. "Yeah, we know. But

still . . . this is kind of gross. No offense."

Coralie gazed at him speculatively for a moment. "None taken, I'm sure," she said coolly.

Then she waved a hand in the air, rather like a conductor giving an orchestra the cue to begin.

Immediately, Kali and Ariadne swam over to join her. The three mermaids turned to face the kayaks and began singing.

Poppy shivered. The song sounded like nothing she had ever heard before. The music was haunting and unearthly; the words slipped away as soon as they were sung, so that they remained frustratingly out of reach. She frowned, concentrating harder. If only she could pick up one or two phrases, something that she could write in her logbook later on. . . .

Her thoughts were interrupted by a mighty splash. Poppy turned to see Henry in the lake, treading water and staring at Kali with a dazed expression.

Kali flashed him a beguiling smile. He began swimming toward her.

"Henry! What are you doing?" Will shouted.

Ariadne began singing again. This time, she was singing a song that seemed to slip up and down the scales. It sounded like golden sun pouring on a meadow of flowers, like a summer breeze floating down a country lane, like cool water rippling over river rocks—

Splash!

Poppy blinked in disbelief. Now Will was in the water, too, and swimming straight for Ariadne.

"Will, Henry, come back!" she shouted. "Get back in the kayak."

But Will and Henry kept swimming with that same dazed look on their faces.

Coralie lazily circled Poppy's kayak. "I don't think they want to leave us," she murmured, her gray-green eyes bright with amusement. "Perhaps all that gross girl stuff is more powerful than they thought. . . ."

Poppy glared at her. "What are you doing to them?"

"Why, nothing," Coralie said innocently.

"We're just singing. Nothing more."

"Right," snapped Nerissa. "And that song will make them swim until they're so tired they can't swim anymore and then they'll drown. Cut it out, Coralie!"

The amused look in Coralie's eyes vanished. "I must have heard you incorrectly, Nerisssa," she said. "Surely you didn't just give me an order? Not when your friends are all in such danger?"

Poppy caught her breath. She looked at Will and Henry, who were doggedly swimming around Ariadne and Kali, and at Franny who was humming to herself as she floated in the water, practicing a flirtatious wave.

"Please stop," said Poppy.

Coralie gave her a long look, as if she was trying to decide what to do.

"Please," Poppy said again. "We need your help."

"Hmm." Coralie tilted her head to one side and smiled faintly. "Well. Since you asked so politely—"

She waved her hand again. Instantly, the singing ended.

Will and Henry stopped swimming. They looked at each other, then glanced around, as if puzzled to find themselves in the water.

"Hey," said Henry, "what happened?"

"Yeah, I don't remember getting out of the kayak," said Will, frowning.

Kali and Ariadne snickered. Coralie contented herself with a cool smile.

"Precisely," she said, flicking a glance at Poppy. "Perhaps you will think twice before you mock mermaids again, hmm?"

"Look, can someone tell us what happened—" Will began.

"Just get back in your kayak!" said Poppy. "I'll explain later."

As Will and Henry swam to their kayak, Kali said, "Come on, Franny. Let's swim over to those boats." She pointed to a few sailboats tacking their way across the water. "They'll be telling the story about how they saw mermaids at the lake for years!"

"Ooh, yes, let's!" said Franny, her eyes sparkling

as she began swimming away. "That sounds like fun!"

"Wait a minute," said Nerissa. "Aren't you forgetting something?"

Franny stopped long enough to give her a bored look. "What?"

"You've got to change places with me," Nerissa snapped.

"Oh, right," said Franny as her attention drifted back to the Jet Ski, which was now roaring toward them. "But you know, I feel as if I'm where I'm supposed to be right now—"

She dove under the water, then reemerged moments later on the other side of the kayak.

Coralie glanced from Franny to Nerissa, a thin smile on her face. "And you certainly look as if you're in your element," she purred. "What would be the harm in staying a mermaid for just a little longer?"

"Coralie!" Nerissa's face was white with shock. "You don't want to keep her with you, do you? I mean, she's a—a mortal."

The older mermaid lifted one shoulder in an elegant shrug. "Well, dear, you were the one who wished to walk on land," she pointed out. "And Franny seems to enjoy being a mermaid. What's the harm in giving you both a day of fun?"

Poppy said, "I don't think that's such a good idea, do you, Franny?"

"What?" asked Franny vaguely.

Ariadne and Kali moved closer to Franny and began swimming lazily around her. Every once in a while, they would cast a slyly amused glance at Poppy.

Franny didn't notice. She was too busy slowly moving her arms back and forth in the water and watching the ripples she made with a rapt expression. "Look, isn't that pretty?"

"Listen to me!" said Poppy sharply. "You were terrified when you turned into a mermaid. So now you want to change back to a girl, right?"

Franny looked up from the water and smiled dreamily. "Sure," she said. "But let's do it tomorrow. I'll meet you in the cove after breakfast and we'll change places then."

"An excellent solution!" said Coralie.

Poppy glanced at Nerissa, who was chewing her lip and frowning. "What do you think?" Poppy asked in a low voice.

Nerissa shrugged. "I guess I can wait one day," she said grudgingly.

"Okay," said Poppy. "Tomorrow after breakfast." She hesitated. "Franny, you will remember, won't you?"

"Of course," Franny said, but she sounded as if her mind was someplace else. "I won't forget, I promise."

And then she dove into the water and disappeared.

Chapter
FOURTEEN

When they got back to the houseboat, Poppy was nervous that her parents would ask if they'd seen any signs that UFOs had landed, such as burned circles on the ground or strange lights in the sky. And she was afraid that they might decide to call Franny, just to make sure that it was all right for her to spend so much time on her new friend's boat.

She shouldn't have worried. As soon as they got back, Mr. Malone pounced.

"We've been waiting for you," he said. He was sitting at a table on the deck and peering down at a half dozen photos. "Just look what I have here!"

They gathered around the table and peered

over his shoulder. Each photo showed a series of blurry lights lined up in a V shape.

"Your mother just developed the photos we took the other night," Mr. Malone said. "Look at that pattern of lights! Aliens are clearly sending us a message. The only question is—what are they trying to tell us?"

There was a short silence as everyone stared blankly at the photos.

"The lights are in a V shape," Mrs. Malone suggested helpfully. "Let's put our thinking caps on. What could that mean?"

"V for Victory?" Poppy suggested.

Mrs. Malone frowned. "What sort of victory?"

Henry brightened. "Maybe they are planning to invade," he said. "And they're planning to win."

"You can't declare victory before you attack," Will said scornfully. "I think that looks like a slice of pie."

"You're just hungry," said Poppy. "That doesn't look anything like a piece of pie."

"It does if you squint," Will insisted. "Maybe

that's what the aliens are saying. They're hungry. And they like pie."

"Okay, if we're going with a food theory, it could also be a slice of pizza," Poppy pointed out.

Will nodded seriously. "So the real question before us is this—is it more likely that an advanced race would travel interstellar distances for a cheese and pepperoni pizza? Or for an apple pie? Our phone lines are open."

Mr. Malone swept the photos together and picked them up. "I can't believe my own offspring are mocking a serious scientific endeavor," he said. "When I was growing up, children had a sense of curiosity. They were filled with wonder at all the mysteries the world had in store. They spent time observing the world around them, noticing the odd, the unusual, the unexpected. . . ."

Poppy had heard this lecture many times before. She glanced over her father's shoulder and saw Franny leap from the water, do a double somersault, and dive back into the lake.

"The strange, the mysterious—" intoned Mr. Malone.

As if to cap off her performance, Franny turned her tail as she hit the water and slapped the surface with a resounding smack. Water flew through the air, wetting everyone on the houseboat deck.

"They didn't dismiss or ignore things that were unusual," went on Mr. Malone, dashing water from his eyes. "They paid *attention*—"

"Dad!" Rolly shouted.

"What?" Mr. Malone snapped.

Rolly was pointing at the empty lake. "I saw it." His eyes were shining with what looked like joy—or, at least, a deep and intense desire to land an enormous fish.

"Saw what?"

"The lake monster! It jumped up in the air, right by the boat."

"Nonsense, Rolly. I told you where these obsessions would lead and I was right. Now you're seeing things. So . . ." Mr. Malone turned back to his reluctant audience. "What was I saying?"

"You were talking about how important it is to pay attention to what's going on around you," Poppy said. She couldn't let herself look at Henry and Will, who were standing behind Mr. Malone, their faces red with suppressed laughter. "Especially if it's strange or unusual."

"Exactly right!" said Mr. Malone. "Excellent observation skills! That's key to being a good scientist. Now, back to our evidence . . ."

He bent over the photos again. When no one else joined him, he stood up, pointed at Will and Henry, and said, "You two. Come over here. I have a job for you."

"We haven't even had dinner yet," Will protested. "And Henry's our guest. I don't think it's fair to make him work."

"It's not work if you enjoy it," said Mr. Malone heartily. "And Henry is now a full-fledged, enthusiastic member of the team! Aren't you, Henry?"

"Yes, sir," Henry said cheerfully.

But Will's face turned pale with dismay as Mr. Malone reached under the table, picked up a cardboard box, and dumped the contents on the table.

"You're kidding!" Will said. "There must be hundreds of photos there."

"Yes, and these are just the ones from last night," Mr. Malone said with some satisfaction. "We may have thousands before we're through. I don't think any UFO investigator has ever managed to collect so much evidence in such a short amount of time. They all need to be logged in, then the time stamp on each photo has to be compared to any abnormal wavelength frequencies picked up by the spectrometer."

Henry gulped, but he was a true and loyal friend. "I'd be glad to help out, Mr. Malone," he said. "With all of us working together, it shouldn't take that long."

"Don't fool yourself," said Will bitterly. "This is just the beginning. There will be hundreds more tomorrow and the day after that and then the day after that—"

"All the more reason to get started right away,"

said Mrs. Malone brightly. "Otherwise, they'll just keep piling up. Why don't I bring you boys some sodas and snacks to hold you until dinner?"

Henry's eyes brightened at that. Will gave a resigned nod and slumped into a chair. He picked up a photo and stared gloomily at it. "Twelve-oh-two a.m.," he said in a hollow tone. "Write that down, Henry. We only have about three hundred more to go."

Poppy caught Nerissa's eye and tilted her head toward the galley. "Nerissa and I will go below and do some online research," she said quickly. "Maybe we could, uh, check out some blogs to see if anyone saw anything in the sky last night. There's a guy in a little town outside Austin who listens to a police band radio and writes a post every time someone calls 911 to report a UFO."

"That would be most useful, Poppy, thank you," Mrs. Malone said. She flashed a brief smile at Poppy, but was quickly distracted by the sight of one hundred worms crawling—slowly but with wormy determination—across the deck.

"Rolly!" she said. "Your worm bucket fell over *again*! How many times have I told you—"

Poppy took advantage of this dramatic moment to grab Nerissa's arm and escape.

It was time, she thought, to come up with a plan.

"I can't believe it," said Nerissa, fuming. "They're luring her!"

Poppy was sitting cross-legged on her bunk, searching the Internet on her laptop. "What are you talking about?"

"Coralie and the others! They're going to convince her to stay with them." Nerissa was sitting on the other end of the bunk. She pulled her legs up under her and glared at Poppy. "Didn't you notice how they started swimming between you and Franny? How they were separating her from you? They're trying to pull you both apart."

"I don't understand," said Poppy, frowning. "Why would they do something like that?"

"Because they're mermaids," Nerissa snapped. "That's what they do."

"But—"

"Look." Nerissa took a deep breath and then spoke very slowly and clearly, as if trying to explain something to a small child. "Mermaids used to lure sailors to their deaths—and that was just for fun! They like making people look like fools. They'll get Franny to leave her family and become one of them, and then they'll spend the next hundred years laughing at her behind her back."

"Franny would never leave us." Poppy's stomach suddenly felt hollow. "Never."

Nerissa gave her a scornful look. "Don't you get it? It won't be up to Franny! I've heard stories—"

She stopped suddenly. Her gaze slid away as if she wanted to look anywhere except at Poppy.

Poppy took a deep breath to calm herself. "Go on," she said. "Tell me."

A fleeting expression crossed Nerissa's face. Poppy shivered. It was the first time she had seen Nerissa look sorry for someone else. It was scarier than anything that had happened so far.

After a moment, Nerissa nodded. "Okay," she

said. "I've heard stories about people who forgot who they were. If they want to, mermaids can make mortals lose every memory, every thought, every dream they ever had when they walked on land. They forget they were ever human. And if that happens to Franny, she might just stay a mermaid . . . forever."

"Oh." Poppy couldn't think of a single thing to say.

Nerissa fell back against a pillow and added, "And Franny is my only hope of turning into a mermaid again. If she refuses to give me my cloak, I'm going to be stuck here forever."

"Oh, well, that's the real problem, isn't it?" Poppy asked, not even bothering to hide the sarcastic edge in her voice. "Forget what Franny's going through; you're worried about being stuck in the human world."

Nerissa blinked several times. "I think that's what Coralie and the others want," she said in a small voice. "I think maybe they like her better than me. . . ."

But Poppy wasn't listening. She had found what she was searching for online.

"Um, Nerissa . . ." she began. She was trying to sound calm, but her voice came out squeaky and scared.

Nerissa turned to look at her. "What's wrong?"

Poppy was still staring at her laptop. "Remember what you told me about how mermaids can only walk on land during a blue moon?"

"Ye-es." Nerissa frowned. "What does that have to do with anything?"

Poppy kept her eyes on the screen as she clicked on another link. "Well, the first night we spent on the houseboat, I saw your lights on shore. That's when you and the others were dancing. That was the first night of the blue moon." She began scrolling through pages on another website. "Then the next day, I met you at the library and you stayed over at our house. That was the second night. And then today, Franny turned into a mermaid. Which means tonight is the third night."

"I can count as well as you," said Nerissa, her voice on edge. "What's wrong?"

"A full moon only lasts for about four days," said Poppy. "What happens if you don't turn back into a mermaid by the time it's ended?"

Nerissa's eyes widened. "I'm not sure," she said. "Do you think—maybe I won't be able to change back, even if I get my cloak?"

"I don't know," said Poppy. "Maybe you'd have to wait until the next blue moon."

"So when would that be, then?" asked Nerissa, biting her lip.

Poppy scanned the article on her screen. "Oh."

"How long?" Nerissa asked.

"It's not so bad," Poppy said in a falsely cheerful voice. "Only another sixteen months . . ."

There was a long silence.

Then Nerissa almost shouted, "You mean I have to spend more than a year as a human being?"

"Shh!" Poppy said, glancing nervously at the door. "What about Franny? By the next blue moon, she'll be fifteen years old."

And who knows what she'll be like by then, after all that time as a mermaid. . . .

She drummed her fingers on her laptop and thought hard for a moment, then said slowly, "You said that mermaids like making humans look like fools. But they don't like it when someone makes fun of them, right?"

"What do you mean?" Nerissa frowned slightly, and a sudden sharp breeze blew the window curtains into Poppy's face.

"You know," said Poppy, batting the curtain away. "They get all . . . huffy."

Nerissa's eyes narrowed and the lightbulb in the bedside lamp popped. "*I* don't," she said. "*I* have a great sense of humor."

"Uh-huh," said Poppy, trying not to roll her eyes. "Like in the library when you kicked that bookshelf and I laughed and suddenly all those dark clouds appeared? Or when you got mad at the mermaid show and a thunderstorm came rolling in? Or when Coralie got angry because she thought Will and Henry were mocking her—"

"Okay, okay," said Nerissa, rather grumpily. "So mermaids like to be treated with dignity and respect. What's wrong with that?"

"Nothing," said Poppy. "But it made me remember something. Hold on a second—"

She reached down to grab a book from the floor. It was *Mermaids in Myth, Legend, and Life*, the book she had found in the library. As she began flipping through it, she said, "I was reading this the other night. There's a story in here about a man who outwitted a mermaid—"

"Impossible," sniffed Nerissa. "Humans aren't smart enough."

Poppy felt a flash of annoyance at that, but she said evenly, "Well, some humans are smarter than others, you know. And if this story is true and if we can figure out how he did it, maybe it will help us."

"If, if, if," muttered Nerissa, but she waved a hand toward the book. "Go ahead, then. It's better than nothing."

Poppy turned back to the book. After a minute,

she said, "Okay, here it is." She scanned the page quickly. "So this story is about a sailor who saw a mermaid sitting on a rock. She was combing her hair and singing and her voice was so beautiful—"

"That he instantly fell in love with her," said Nerissa impatiently. "All the stories start that way. And then the sailor forgets that he can't swim, jumps into the sea to be with her, and drowns. The end."

"Hold on," said Poppy. She turned the page. "This sailor happened to be a very careful person. So instead of just flinging himself over the railing, he leaned over to see how far away the water was—"

"She must not have been much of a singer," muttered Nerissa.

"Anyway," said Poppy firmly. "The sea happened to be very smooth that day, so he saw his own reflection in the water. As soon as he recognized himself, the spell was broken."

There was a long silence, then Nerissa's eyes met Poppy's.

"So what are you thinking?" she asked.

For the first time all day, a grin appeared on Poppy's face. "I think we've only got one more day to turn Franny back into a girl and you back into a mermaid," she said. "And I think I'm beginning to have what could end up being a brilliant idea. Even if I am just a human."

Nerissa bit her lip, then she started smiling, too. "Well, you are one of the smarter ones, I have to admit," she said. "So let's hear it. . . ."

And together, Poppy and Nerissa cooked up the perfect plan to get Franny back.

"Franny!" Poppy called out. Her voice echoed over the water. "Where are you?"

She paused and listened hard, but all she heard was the sound of waves lapping against the side of her kayak and a distant bird twittering cheerfully.

"We're not going to find her by yelling her name," said Nerissa from the seat behind her.

"Well, we can't just paddle around the lake hoping we run into her, either," snapped Poppy. "Maybe we should just go to the cove and wait—"

Then she heard the faint sound of a girl's laugh float over the water.

"Wait, did you hear that?" Poppy asked Nerissa. "Was that her? It sounded like it came from those rocks by the shore—"

The laugh sounded again, a little louder. This time it seemed to come from behind the kayak.

Poppy twisted around, squinting against the glare of the sun. All she saw was calm, still water.

"They're playing tricks on us," said Nerissa. "That's probably Kali. She knows how to throw her voice so it sounds like it's coming from in front of you, then behind you, then over to the side—"

"Why would they do that?" asked Poppy. "They must know how worried we are."

Nerissa gave a skeptical snort. "I keep telling you—"

"I know, I know," said Poppy. "They're mermaids." She took a deep breath, then shouted, "If this is your idea of a joke, it's not funny. We just want to see Franny and make sure she's all right."

There was no answer.

Poppy sighed and looked at her watch. Mr. Malone had been so enthusiastic about the UFO analysis that Will and Henry had done the night before that he had laid down the law—everyone was ordered to help out as soon as breakfast was over.

Darting glances had flown among Will and Henry and Poppy when they realized that there was no way they would all be able to go back to the cove together. After a long, whispered argument, Poppy had been deputized to check on Franny, as long as she promised to return as quickly as possible. They had decided that Nerissa should be the one to confess that she had accidentally left the Geiger counter at the cove (Poppy knew that Mrs. Malone would never lecture a guest about carelessness). Their cover story accepted, the two had set off to find Franny.

Now time was ticking on, Franny was nowhere to be seen, and Will and Henry were probably getting more annoyed by the minute as they waited for Poppy and Nerissa's return.

Poppy tried to stay calm. She sat very still and thought as hard as she could about where Franny might be. Her kayak rocked gently on the water. A drop of sweat rolled down her nose. In the distance, she could hear the sound of singing. . . .

Singing!

Poppy turned her head sharply. "Did you hear that?" she whispered.

"Shh," said Nerissa.

Together, they held their breath, trying to figure out where the sound was coming from. A slight breeze seemed to make the voices waft into hearing. But then, as soon as Poppy caught the tune, the breeze would shift and the music would become fainter.

"It's coming from that direction." Nerissa pointed past the cove where Poppy had first seen the mermaids.

Poppy tilted her head and listened hard. "I think you're right." She took a deep breath and said, "Okay, remember the plan. We have to make sure Coralie thinks it's all her idea—"

"I know what we have to do!" snapped Nerissa.

"Good," said Poppy. "Let's go."

Slowly, they began paddling along the shoreline, following the sound of singing. A few times, the sound seemed to disappear altogether, and Poppy's stomach would clench, but then the breeze would pick up and she'd hear the voices once more.

Finally, they rounded a bend and saw another inlet. Poppy guided the kayak through the opening and down a narrow stream, while Nerissa kept paddling. Then the stream widened and they found that they were gliding into another cove with several limestone boulders along the shoreline. And on each boulder sat a mermaid, singing.

Ariadne was plaiting her hair into a long golden braid. Kali was gazing raptly into a hand mirror framed in silver. Coralie was holding one slender hand in front of her, smugly admiring her fingernails. And Franny was combing her hair with an ivory comb. All of them were singing the strange, wandering tune that Poppy had heard and all of them had the half-smiling expression of someone who is quite pleased with the way she looks.

Franny, Poppy noticed uneasily, seemed right at home.

"Are you okay?" Poppy's voice was sharper

than she had intended, but it had the right effect.

Franny blinked, as if she were waking from a dream. She turned her head and looked blankly at Poppy. Then she frowned, as if she were trying to remember who Poppy was.

Or maybe, Poppy thought with a shiver, she was trying to remember who *Franny* was.

After a long, long pause, Franny said, "Of course. I'm fine. Ariadne and Kali and I are having such fun."

Finally, she smiled—but that smile was sly and secretive, as if she were amused by a joke that only she understood. It didn't look like Franny at all.

Poppy said, "Well, I'm glad you're enjoying yourself, but—"

"I can't believe it!" Nerissa burst out, glaring at Kali and Ariadne. "You're the ones who made fun of me because I was interested in mortals. Why do you want to hang out with *her*?"

Kali raised an eyebrow and said sweetly, "Franny may be mortal, but she's got a mermaid's soul."

"Yes," Ariadne added. "She's one of us, deep down inside."

"She is *not*," Poppy and Nerissa said together.

"No, really, I think I could have some mermaid blood in me," said Franny, her blue eyes wide. "Maybe generations ago, my great-great-great-grandmother was a mermaid who was courted by a handsome young man and they had children and the mermaid genes were passed down to me—"

"Which is why you spend so much time taking baths," Poppy said sarcastically. "Really, that explains so much."

"It does, doesn't it?" said Franny, completely missing the point.

"You are not a mermaid," said Nerissa through gritted teeth. *"I am."*

Ariadne slipped off her rock into the water and, with a graceful flick of her tail, swam over to their kayak. Poppy couldn't help noticing that this meant that Ariadne was now between her and Franny. She shot a quick glance at Franny. Was it her imagination, or did Franny's expression when she looked at Poppy seem more blank?

"Now Nerissa," Ariadne crooned, "you didn't really like being a mermaid, did you? You were always complaining about how you hated dancing—"

"And playing tricks on people," added Kali.

"And singing," Ariadne said.

"And Franny, on the other hand—" Kali smiled warmly at her.

"Franny," Ariadne finished, "is a natural."

"That's true," said Franny, preening. "Everything Ariadne and Kali have been teaching me about mermaid ways just seems to make so much sense to me!"

Poppy shuddered, but she tried to sound casual. "Really. Like what?"

"Oh, you know." Franny lifted one shoulder in a tiny shrug. It reminded Poppy of someone, but she couldn't think who. "How to make a face pack out of algae. How to follow the stars at night. How to sing so sweetly that sailors want to follow you anywhere—"

"That sounds pretty dangerous," said Poppy. She knew she sounded prim, but she couldn't help it. "You could cause a boating accident or something."

This caused another series of sly smiles among Franny and the other two mermaids that Poppy found both unsettling and extremely annoying. Unsettling because the smiles were colder than any human smile she'd ever seen. And annoying because, once again, Poppy felt as if Franny and her new friends were a little club and the only person who didn't belong was her.

"Oh, I think it might be funny to watch a boat tip over or run aground," Franny said airily.

Kali clapped her hands in delight. "Oh yes, you're right, it's quite humorous! Every time it happens, we just laugh and laugh!"

"It wasn't that much fun when it happened to us," said Poppy, remembering the night of their boat accident. "You should think about how other people feel, too, you know."

Franny flashed an amused look at Kali and

Ariadne. "She's very proper, isn't she?"

They laughed, and Poppy felt herself becoming more frightened, which only made her angrier.

"Franny, please." Poppy didn't care about winning this argument, but she felt somehow that if she did—if she managed to convince Franny that it wasn't right to play tricks on people—that she might also help Franny remember who she was. "Someone could get hurt."

Franny tossed her head. "Oh, who would be hurt?" she said. "Mortals?"

Poppy caught her breath at the disdain she heard in Franny's voice. "Well, yes, people," she said carefully. "People like us."

Franny cocked her head, as if she couldn't quite grasp what Poppy was saying. "Like us?"

"Yes, like us! Like you, me, Will, Rolly!" Poppy shouted, finally losing patience. "Like Mom and Dad."

"Oh yes, of course." Franny said vaguely, as if she was trying to remember who Poppy was talking about.

A tiny shiver ran down Poppy's spine.

She glanced at Nerissa. This was her cue.

There was a split-second pause. Poppy felt her stomach lurch at the thought that Nerissa had forgotten what to say—but then Nerissa tossed her head and said with great disdain, "That's okay. I don't need to turn back into a mermaid. I can join the mermaid show. They'll give me a tail to put on and I'll swim around the lake just like I used to."

As one, the three mermaids turned toward her. Their eyes were suddenly sharp, watchful.

"What are you talking about?" asked Coralie.

Poppy glanced at Nerissa and gave a little nod. Nerissa reached into her pocket and pulled out the brochure for the mermaid show.

This is it, Poppy thought, crossing her fingers and holding her breath. Everything depended on the mermaids reacting the way she thought they would. . . .

"Here," Nerissa said, holding out the brochure. "Look at this."

Coralie snatched it from her hand. A small

crease appeared on her forehead as she stared at it.

"What is this?" she asked with a hiss of displeasure. "Humans pretending to be . . . mermaids?"

"Exactly!" Poppy said brightly. "The show is starting this afternoon."

"This is . . . unfortunate," Coralie said. It was just a murmur, but Poppy felt the hairs on her arms stand up. The air seemed to chill several degrees. Her kayak rocked as the ripples on the water suddenly turned into waves.

"What harm does it do?" Poppy asked. "So what if people think that mermaids—"

"Have tea parties? Swim in parades? Wave flags?" Coralie asked in a dangerous voice.

"Well . . . yes," Poppy said. "It sounds like fun, doesn't it?"

Thunderclouds formed on the horizon.

"Fun?" Coralie spat out. "To watch mortals pretend to be mermaids—and make mermaids look like fools?"

There was a distant roll of thunder.

"But the audience loves it," Poppy said

helpfully. "Especially when they play a game of touch football—"

Lightning crashed. Wind whipped across the lake. Coralie's hair rose into the air and writhed around her head as she turned to Kali, Ariadne, and Franny.

"This show," she said in a steely voice, "must be stopped. *By any means necessary.*"

Chapter
SIXTEEN

"Are you sure this is going to work?" Will asked nervously.

"It better," Poppy answered shortly. She was lying on the ground and tugging on an orange mermaid tail. It was made of spandex and so far she had only managed to pull it up as far as her knees. "This is horrible! Who invented this stupid costume?"

"Some human," Nerissa snapped. She was struggling with a purple tail. "Obviously. I told you they aren't that smart."

Poppy stopped to wipe the sweat off her face. She was wearing her swimsuit, which was bright pink. She now realized, too late, that the combination of a pink swimsuit and an orange tail was not going to help her slip into the mermaid parade unnoticed.

"This is the hardest part," she assured Nerissa. "Once we get our costumes on, everything will be fine."

Will was standing at the door of the mermaid hut, keeping watch. He glanced over his shoulder and said, "Hurry up! The show's going to start any minute."

Poppy took in a deep breath, then pulled hard on the stretchy fabric. "There!" she said triumphantly. "I've got it on."

"Me, too," said Nerissa. "Now what?"

"Now we just need to wait until the rest of the mermaids take their places and sneak in with them," said Poppy with a confidence she didn't quite feel. "Piece of cake."

"Are you sure you can breathe okay underwater?" Henry looked concerned.

"The mermaids have air hoses," Poppy reassured him. "And I took scuba diving lessons when we lived in Laguna Beach. We'll be fine. Will, do you have the mirror?"

Will pulled a small hand mirror out of his backpack and handed it to her. "Are you sure you can get close enough to Franny to use this?" he asked.

Poppy tugged on her tail, then tucked the mirror into the waistband. "Look, we've gone over this a million times," she said as patiently as she could. "Nerissa will swim right next to her and keep edging her over in my direction. As soon as I can, I'll take it out and hold it in front of her face. She'll remember who she is and that will be that."

There was a short silence in the changing hut.

"Yeah," said Will. "So like I keep saying, we need a Plan B."

Poppy tried walking a few steps and immediately fell over.

"Even if Plan A doesn't work, she'll still be in the lake," Henry pointed out as he helped Poppy get to her feet. "It's not like Franny's in the Atlantic Ocean. We could find her again if we search hard enough—"

"People have been searching for that big catfish for years," Nerissa pointed out. "He's still out there somewhere. And"—she lifted her chin proudly—"no one has ever caught even a glimpse of us."

Us. The mermaids, living in a lake for centuries without anyone noticing . . . and now Franny was about to join their ranks. . . .

"Look," said Poppy. "This is our last chance. If Franny decides to disappear, she'll be lost forever."

As soon as they saw the mermaid show performers heading for the changing station, Will and Henry slipped away with whispered good-byes and good lucks.

Poppy and Nerissa tried to look casual as the door opened and a half dozen young women entered the room, chattering and laughing.

"Honey, I'm beginning to think I've been doing this mermaid gig a little too long," said one in a syrupy drawl. She had dark hair that had been teased into a pile on top of her head and then hair sprayed until it barely moved. "I swear I'm going to find webs between my toes one of these days."

"That would be brilliant, Allyson!" said another girl. She was small and looked like an arty type, with long, flowing hair and two small earrings in each ear. "It would show that you were really getting into your role."

"And people would point and laugh any time I went to the pool," Allyson said dryly. "Thanks, Chloe, but I'll pass."

Poppy could feel Nerissa stiffen, so she put her hand on Nerissa's arm to calm her.

"Let it go," Poppy whispered. "We've got an act to do, remember?"

Nerissa relaxed enough to nod, just as the eyes of the performers turned their way.

"Well, hi, there!" said Allyson. "Don't y'all look adorable!"

Poppy gritted her teeth. The last time she had been called adorable, she was playing a flying monkey in a school production of *The Wizard of Oz*. And she had only been five years old.

She forced a smile on her face. "Thank you,"

she said. "You look great, too. Very, um, authentic."

This made the mermaids laugh.

"Well, it's true that some of us did lots of research for this role," said Chloe, pulling a spandex tail out of her backpack.

The other mermaids rolled their eyes at this.

"Chloe's an actress," one of them explained. "You'd think this was Shakespeare, the way she studied her part! I'm Shannon, by the way." She pointed to another girl with brown curly hair and an impish smile. "And that's Crystal."

"Hey, it's important to know the character you're playing," Chloe said good-humoredly. "You have to know how a mermaid waves and when she'll wink at someone and when she won't and what she thinks about all day under the sea—"

Poppy's eyes met Nerissa's and they shared a secret smile.

If you only knew, Poppy thought. All your questions could be answered right here. . . .

But then the conversation moved on, to gossip

and talk about movies that were opening that weekend and who was interested in going out for dinner after the show. The other mermaids sat on benches around the room, pulling on their costumes as they talked. They were a lot better at this than Poppy and Nerissa, probably because they'd had more practice.

"But hey, what are you two doing here, anyway?" asked Allyson.

Poppy took a breath. Now it was time for her to act. "We're going to be in the show today," she said with a big smile.

The other performers looked at one another.

"You are?" said Shannon. "Bud McCray—he's the guy who runs the show—he didn't tell us anything about that—"

"It was a last-minute thing," said Poppy smoothly. "Just for this one performance."

"That doesn't sound right," she said, frowning. "I mean, you both look cute and all that, but we had to train for months—"

"Yeah, the swimming isn't as easy as it looks,"

said Crystal. "And you have to know where the air hoses are hidden and how to take little sips of air as you swim by—"

"We know how to do all that," Nerissa said abruptly. She added, in a firm voice that did not invite any argument, "We took lessons."

A few of the mermaids looked unconvinced, but just then there was a loud knock on the door and the sound of someone shouting, "Five-minute warning! Five minutes to showtime!"

Allyson looked at Chloe and shrugged. "I guess Bud knows what he's doing," she said.

"Well, he sure knows how to please the crowd," Chloe said. She turned to Poppy and Nerissa. "I bet you two will be a sensation! But listen, if you get into any trouble out there, just swim for the surface, okay? Don't worry about the show."

"We won't," Poppy promised.

"That's right," Crystal said. "Even if something unexpected happens, the audience always thinks we planned it that way."

* * *

Poppy and Nerissa hopped with the other performers to a hidden spot behind the changing station. One by one, they slipped into the water and swam toward the glass-bottom boats, which were arranged in a circle about fifty yards off shore. Just before they reached the boats—and before any of the audience members crowded on the boats could see them—each mermaid dove down, swimming toward a formation of rocks on the bottom of the lake.

Poppy had spent some time researching the mermaid show. She knew that several tanks of air were cleverly hidden in those rocks. The performers could dive down anytime they needed a breath and take a sip of air from the hoses attached to the tanks. She also knew that, in order to perform in the show, mermaids had to be able to hold their breath for two-and-a-half minutes, so she and Nerissa had practiced.

It turned out that Nerissa, even without her tail, had kept some of her mermaid abilities. Although she couldn't breathe underwater anymore, she was still able to hold her breath for ten minutes at a stretch.

Poppy, on the other hand, was gasping for breath after a minute.

I'm okay, she thought with a confidence she didn't quite feel. I know where all the air hoses are hidden. If I need air, I'll just swim over to those rocks and take a little sip.

Now they formed a circle with the other mermaids. Poppy looked up. She could see the glass-bottom boats above them; she could even see curious faces peering down. Somewhere up there, she knew, Will and Henry had joined Mr. and Mrs. Malone and Rolly on one of the glass-bottom boats. They had all bought tickets for the show that had everyone on the lake talking.

Allyson raised her hand and pointed. One by one, the mermaids swam to the spot where the audience on the boats and on the dock could see them.

They swam in a long line, as if they were in a parade. Mermaid Shannon went first, holding a pole with a Texas state flag. The edges of the flag had been stiffened with wire, so it looked as if it were rippling in a strong breeze. The other mermaids swam after her with strong, powerful strokes, smiling up at the glass-bottom boats and waving cheerfully.

Even underwater, Poppy could hear the cheers. She swam down to the rocks, took a quick breath of air, and followed the mermaids out.

It was much harder to swim with spandex wrapping her legs, so she settled on lurking in the background and watching the show. Once in a while, she even remembered to smile. Most of the time, though, she was too busy watching the fake mermaids—and wondering when the real mermaids would show up—to think about performing.

Nerissa, on the other hand, joined in as if she'd been in front of an audience all her life.

When Allyson, Shannon, Chloe, and Crystal swam in a circle and drank bottles of soda, smiling and winking at the audience, Nerissa juggled two bottles and then popped the caps off. When

251

the carbonated soda sprayed through the water, the crowd burst into applause.

While the other mermaids sat at a table and drank tea from fine china cups, Nerissa sipped hers while turning slow, graceful loop-de-loops in the water.

The mermaids performed underwater ballets, played touch football, and even pretended to strum guitars as part of a mermaid band—and Nerissa was always right in the middle, managing to steal the show.

All the performers timed their trips to the air hoses perfectly, so that the audience's attention was always on the show. No one noticed when one or two mermaids slipped away to get a breath of air. And none of the mermaids noticed that Nerissa never had to use the air hose at all.

Poppy would have enjoyed being a part of this spectacle if she weren't so worried about Franny. The plan depended on Coralie feeling so insulted by the mermaid show that she would try to disrupt it—and on Coralie being so focused on what she was doing that Poppy could get close enough to Franny to break the mermaid spell. But they had reached the salute to Texas heroes (the show's finale), and nothing had happened.

Poppy glanced at Nerissa and gave her a questioning look. Nerissa shrugged and shook her head.

It was hard for Poppy to read Nerissa's expression underwater, but she thought she looked upset.

Of course she does, Poppy thought, checking her watch. We only have a few hours left before the moon rises.

And when that happened, she knew they would see a moon that was slightly less than full. Which would mean the blue moon was over, and there would be no going back for Franny.

For a moment, Poppy let herself think about how she would tell her parents what had happened. She allowed herself a horrible moment of imagining how they would react, and an even more horrible moment of thinking about how she would feel to know that she had lost Franny, perhaps forever. . . .

And then she felt a swirl of water around her.

She looked at Nerissa and saw her pointing, wide eyed, at something behind her.

Poppy turned to see the real mermaids, led by Coralie, moving in swiftly.

Ariadne swept into the midst of the mermaid show and grabbed a soda from Mermaid Crystal.

Kali used her tail to sweep aside the tea table and knock a cup from Mermaid Shannon's hand.

Coralie swam in fast, furious circles, creating a vortex that upended the props the performers had been using. The tea table tipped over and sank to the bottom of the lake. The crate of sodas overturned, freeing the bottles which then spun end over end in the underwater currents. The guitars and footballs and Texas state flag all floated to the surface of the water.

And then, at last, Poppy saw Franny. She gleefully swam through the chaos, turning somersaults, her blond hair flowing behind her.

Nerissa swam up fast on her left. For a moment, it looked as if they might collide—then, with a quick movement of her tail, Franny changed direction and headed straight toward Poppy as the crowd on the glass-bottom boat applauded and cheered.

This, Poppy knew, was her moment. She swam down to the air hose, keeping one eye on Franny.

All she had to do was take a nice, deep breath of air, then move in front of Franny, get her attention, and hold up the mirror. If even a little bit of the old Franny remained, she wouldn't be able to resist looking in it. . . .

Poppy stubbornly refused to think about what would happen if none of the old Franny still existed.

She got to the rock formation and reached for the hose. . . .

But at that very moment, Ariadne came toward her, smiling with glee as she chased a terrified Allyson. As she swam by Poppy, her powerful tail flexed and slapped Poppy in the face.

The force of it knocked Poppy away from the rock formation. What was worse, it knocked the air hose out of her mouth.

She made a grab for it, but it was too late.

She held her breath and watched as the hose floated away.

Her heart pounding, Poppy tried to swim back to the rocks, looking frantically for another hose. But it was too late. Her lungs were bursting. If she didn't get air soon, she could drown. . . .

Swim for the surface if anything goes wrong. That's what Chloe had said—and that, of course, was the smart thing to do.

But then Poppy saw Franny, just a few yards away, still doing flips and somersaults and twists as the crowd applauded.

I have to get over to her, Poppy thought. I can hold my breath for a few more seconds. I just have to grab her arm and let her see me—

At that moment, just as if Franny could hear her thoughts, she turned and met Poppy's gaze.

With her last bit of strength, Poppy pulled the mirror from her waistband and started to swim toward Franny—and then, someone grabbed her arm and yanked her up.

Startled, Poppy turned to see Chloe pulling

her to the surface. Chloe was pointing up, toward the sun and the sky and the air, and nodding encouragingly.

Everything's going to be all right, Chloe seemed to be saying. Just hold on. . . .

No! Poppy thought, struggling to get free. This is my last chance!

She glanced down just in time to see the little mirror spinning toward the bottom of the lake, flashing back glints of sunlight as it fell deeper and deeper into the water.

Wait! Poppy thought to herself. I have to get the mirror; it's my last chance to save Franny—

Chloe may have looked slight, but she was stronger than Poppy. It only took a few seconds for them to make it to the top. In fact, they went so fast that Poppy could feel her mermaid tail, which had never been that secure in the first place, slipping off her legs.

Poppy took a big gulp of air. Her feet were still caught in the spandex, so she kicked it off. It rose to the surface, where it floated on the water, nothing more than a piece of stretchy orange material covered with a few spangles.

"What do you think you were doing down there?" Chloe asked sharply. "You could have drowned!"

"You . . . don't understand," Poppy gasped. "My sister . . ."

"Hold on," Chloe said under her breath. She waved to the audience, who had turned away from watching the underwater action to stare at this new plot twist.

"Don't worry, folks, we've got a newbie here," she called out cheerfully. She held up the tail and added, "And she's going to have quite a tale to tell when she gets home!"

Everyone chuckled, then turned around to continue watching the underwater show.

Poppy blinked water out of her eyes until she could see clearly once more. And what she saw was Rolly standing at the railing of the glass-bottom, his fishing pole in hand. He was not trying to get closer to the viewing area. Instead, he was staring fixedly at the waves, every line of his body tense.

As Poppy treaded water, she saw Mr. and Mrs. Malone spot the boat's captain and eagerly push through the crowd to corner him in the stern.

Quickly, she ducked down until only her nose was above water, hoping that her parents hadn't seen her. After a moment, as she watched her parents begin talking excitedly to the captain, she realized that she needn't have worried. Poppy swam closer to the boat so she could hear their conversation.

"Have you ever seen anything extremely unusual at the bottom of this lake?" Mr. Malone was asking.

"You mean, like junked-out old cars?" asked the captain. "Because some people will dump them here, even though it's illegal. *And* dangerous. *And* environmentally unfriendly—"

"Terrible! And so thoughtless!" agreed Mrs. Malone. "But we were thinking of something a little different. Perhaps you have—oh, I don't know—spotted pieces of mysterious spacecraft?"

The captain's smile disappeared. "Er, I don't think—"

"Maybe twisted chunks of metal that happen to glow in the dark?" suggested Mr. Malone.

"No, I would have remembered that," said the captain, trying to edge away.

"Or possibly evidence of interstellar crashes?" Mrs. Malone added brightly. "I've heard that tiny alien corpses sometimes bob to the surface a few days after an incident. The government covers it up, of course, but the stories always get out eventually—"

"Ah, I think I need to correct our course a few degrees . . . if you'll excuse me," said the captain, hurrying off.

Even in the midst of her worry, Poppy was struck by the idea that she really had to admire her parents. They never gave up their quest for evidence of the paranormal—but they were always searching for the wrong thing and looking in the wrong direction. . . .

Like right now, for example, they were missing

their daughter, who had turned into a mermaid and was performing a triple flip half gainer on the other side of the boat to oohs and aahs from the crowd.

As the applause died down, Poppy saw Will and Henry push their way through the crowd to stand behind Rolly at the railing.

Will looked at her, raising his shoulders and lifting his hands, palm up. He mouthed the words: *What happened?*

Poppy cautiously swam toward the boat, keeping her head as low as possible in case Mr. or Mrs. Malone happened to glance in her direction. When she got close enough, Will and Henry pulled her up and she landed on the deck, accidentally splashing a family who were craning their necks to see through the glass bottom of the boat.

"What went on down there?" Will asked under his breath.

"I'm sorry!" she whispered. "The plan didn't work! Franny saw me, but it was like she didn't even know who I was—"

She gulped and felt tears come to her eyes. "I think"—she paused and blinked hard—"I think she's forgotten all about us."

"Okay, don't cry," said Will.

"I'm not crying," Poppy snapped. "I never cry, you know I never cry—"

"All right, fine, just don't do that weird thing where your eyes get all wet," said Will. "What happened to Nerissa?"

Poppy gasped. "I don't know," she said. "Isn't that terrible? I'm a terrible friend! I was so focused on trying to get close to Franny and hold up the mirror, I completely lost track—" Her voice wavered embarrassingly. Poppy stopped and blinked several times.

"Okay, okay, don't get all upset," said Will quickly. "We'll just have to move on to Plan B."

"Will!" Poppy felt a surge of annoyance, which was a good thing. Anger, she knew, was a way to fend off other emotions, like the feeling you were about to cry, which of course she wasn't because she never did. "There is no Plan B! We only had one plan, this plan, Plan A—the one that just ended in disaster!"

"Maybe if we all waved to Franny?" Henry suggested hopefully. "Maybe if she looked up and saw us all? Maybe that would work?"

If Will had made that idiotically optimistic suggestion, Poppy would have treated it with the scorn it deserved. But Henry was her friend, not her brother, so she tried to be polite.

"Yeah," Poppy said dully, her shoulders slumping. "Maybe . . ."

"Poppy," said a voice at her elbow.

She glanced down to see Rolly, still staring intently at the water.

"Yes, what is it, Rolly?" she sighed.

He pointed. "I think I can see Mugwump."

She followed his gaze. It was harder to see the mermaids underwater from the railing, but occasionally a scaly, spangled body would flash by, looking for all the world like a giant fish.

"Sure," she said, her thoughts going back to her parents and what she was going to tell them about how and why Franny had disappeared. "Good for you, Rolly. You finally found him."

She didn't see Rolly's small eyes narrow and become even smaller and more intense.

"Yup," he said with resolve. "And I'm going to catch him."

With that, he reached back with his fishing pole and snapped it forward. The fishing lure sailed across the water just as Franny somersaulted through the air.

"Aggh!" She clapped her hand to her head, then belly flopped back into the water.

Rolly pressed his lips. "I wanted to catch *Mugwump*," he complained. "Not Franny."

The fishing line whirred as Franny dove down into the water.

"She's going to break my fishing line," Rolly said, disgruntled. "Franny always spoils everything."

Poppy's eyes lit up. "No, she doesn't, Rolly," she said. "In fact, this is perfect! You're doing a brilliant job. Just be careful"—she reached over to take the fishing pole from Rolly—"not to lose her."

Rolly twitched the pole away from her. "Leave me alone," he said, his eyes fixed on the spot where Franny had disappeared. "I *know* how to fish."

He began reeling in the line. Poppy watched, holding her breath, as the line stretched out. If the line breaks, she thought, Franny will be gone. . . .

Just as she thought that, the line went slack.

Poppy heard Will and Henry groan. Her heart sank.

And then Franny burst out of the water, only a yard away. She glared at Rolly.

"You are the brattiest little brother in the world!" she yelled. "I was having fun and now you've ruined everything!"

Her eyes flashed as she caught sight of Poppy. "And I can't believe that you put on that silly costume and made a spectacle of yourself in front of all these people! It's bad enough that Mom and Dad embarrass me on a daily basis, but now you're doing that, too. I don't know how I'll ever make friends when I have a family like this—and just look at what you've done to my hair!"

At that moment, Nerissa burst through the surface of the water. "Sounds like someone has remembered who she really is," she called out to Poppy. "Can we not finish off our plan, then?"

Poppy glanced at Will, a huge smile on her face. He was grinning, too.

"Bad-tempered, self-centered, and vain," he said. "That's our Franny."

"Yeah," Poppy said happily. "She's back."

EPILOGUE

"**I**'ll never think about mermaids the same way after this," said Poppy.

"Neither will I," said Henry.

"If I'm really lucky, I'll never think of mermaids ever again in my whole life," muttered Will. "I don't know what it is about Austin, but it seems like there's always something weird happening here that ends up causing us a lot of trouble."

"Oh, come on, stop complaining," said Poppy happily. "Let's go find Franny."

Together, they ran to the mermaid changing station. They could hear the show mermaids talking in loud, agitated voices inside.

"But where did they come from?" Chloe asked plaintively. "I didn't even know there *was* another mermaid show in this area!"

"And why would they ruin our show like that?" asked Shannon.

"Maybe someone wants to put us out of business," said Allyson. "Maybe that guy, what's-his-name, the one with the diving pig."

"Or maybe this was all a publicity stunt dreamed up by Bud McCray," Crystal suggested darkly. "It would be just like him to hire another mermaid crew on the sly and not tell us what he had planned. . . ."

Just then, Franny came walking up the path from the lake. When she caught sight of Poppy, Will, and Henry, she stopped and gave them a quizzical look.

"Oh, hi," she said.

"Are you okay?" asked Poppy. "You sound . . . different."

Franny cocked her head and frowned. "I feel different," she said slowly.

"What do you mean?" asked Will.

"I thought . . . I almost imagined . . . I could have sworn, well"—Franny laughed lightly, embarrassed—"I feel as if I've been living as a mermaid for the last few days."

There was utter silence. No one knew how to respond to this.

"How strange," Poppy said at last.

"Very odd," commented Will.

"Peculiar," said Henry.

"I know." A tiny crease appeared on Franny's forehead. "It must have been a dream," she said. "But it seemed so *real*. . . ."

It wasn't until much later that Poppy, Will, and Henry found out exactly what had happened. They had returned to the houseboat, where Mr. Malone had insisted that everyone help recalibrate the telescopes.

After dinner, Franny had drifted off to bed as soon as the meal was over, saying that she was too tired to even think about taking a shower (this had concerned Mrs. Malone so much that she insisted on taking Franny's temperature).

Then Mr. and Mrs. Malone combined forces to put Rolly to bed (an operation that required capturing Rolly after three separate attempts to dash back on deck). Exhausted, Mr. and Mrs. Malone had retired to their bedroom, even though the sun hadn't even set yet. Finally, Poppy, Will, and Henry could be on their own.

"We're going to take the kayaks out, all right?" Poppy had called to her parents.

"Of course, my darlings, just be careful," Mrs. Malone called back through a huge yawn. In the background, Mr. Malone could already be heard snoring. "Be back in an hour and knock on our door to let us know you're home. . . ."

Her voice faded as she drifted off to sleep.

Quietly, they lowered the kayaks and slipped away toward the cove.

"Do you think we'll be able to find Nerissa?" asked Henry in a hushed voice.

"I don't know; it's a big lake," said Will.

Poppy added, "And she may not want us to find her. I don't think she's as fond of humans as she used to be—"

Before she could finish her sentence, there was a swell of water, the sense of a large object moving under her, and Poppy's kayak tipped over.

Holding her breath, Poppy pulled her legs out of the kayak. As she broke the surface, gasping for air, she saw that Will and Henry had also been tipped over and were now treading water and peering around them.

Will said, a little nervously, "I sure hope that was a mermaid and not Mugwump—"

The water behind him seemed to explode. Nerissa threw herself into the air, performing a jubilant triple somersault before landing back in the water with a giant splash.

"Of course it's not Mugwump, you idjit," she said, beaming. "Oh, it feels good to have fins and scales again!"

Poppy smiled in relief. "How did you make the change?" she asked. "And why doesn't

Franny remember anything?"

Nerissa grinned. She swam two fast circles around the kayaks before stopping to answer Poppy's question.

"Once Franny remembered who she was, it was easy," said Nerissa. "We just nipped to a nice quiet little inlet and I told her how to turn her tail into a cloak. She handed it to me—"

"And turned back into the most annoying sister on the planet," interrupted Will.

"To be fair, she was pretty annoying as a mermaid, too," Poppy pointed out.

"But why can't Franny remember what happened to her?" asked Henry.

Nerissa's eyes sparkled with mischief. "Well, let's just call it mermaid magic," she said. "If we can make a human forget she was once mortal, we can make her forget that she was once a mermaid, too."

"Just as well," said Will. "It's already hard enough to get in the bathroom with her around."

Nerissa flipped over to float on her back, smiling

blissfully at the stars. "Ah, the water feels so nice," she said. "I'll never, ever wish to be a human being again."

She glanced over at Poppy, Will, and Henry. "No offense."

"Of course not," said Poppy. "But . . . does this mean we'll never see you again?"

Nerissa's smile widened. "Of course not," she said, deliberately echoing Poppy's words. "We're friends now, aren't we? But just remember"—she winked at them—"you'd better watch out if you hear me singing!"

And with that, she did a backflip, waved goodbye with her tail, and swam away.